The Tortures of Thomas Darkne

Luk

*Thomas Darkne is a being of great ...
From a very young age, he discovered the art
and through years of training he now uses it
to his advantage... to torture and kill all those
he deems lesser then him. Enter his twisted,
crazy world where killing is his pleasure and
eating human flesh is his pass time. Where
he cuts his hair with a chainsaw and gels it
with the blood of his many victims!!*

*The reader should expect gore, strong
violence, scenes of a disturbing nature,
sadistic laughs, great characters, vampires,
magicians, spiders, dragons, death and
much, much more...*

1

Books by Luke Crook...

TORTURES OF THOMAS DARKNE

TRAILS OF DEATH

QUESTION MARKS

(And still to be published...)

I'M THE GOOD GUY

WELCOME TO GOREDOM

IMMORTAL COMBAT 1 AND 2

THE HISTORY OF THOMAS DARKNE

MASTER DARKNESS 1 AND 2

Self Published by Luke J.J. Crook on the LuLu Publishing website

(lulu.com)

First published 2014

ISBN: 978-1-291-72264-2

Contents

The Tortures of

Thomas Darkne

Torture one: Darkne madness

In this part you will be introduced to Thomas Darkne for the first time as he decides to make the life of a bored teenage boy called Lee more interesting… by doing what Darkne does best.

Chapter one: Signs

I woke up yawning and frowning angrily at the fact that my body was actually giving me no choice but to get up, I couldn't simply shut down for even just another five minutes. My body reluctantly dragged itself up and I forced on a black jumper which was lazily slung across my bedroom floor along with the rest of the towering piles of clothes that I couldn't be bothered to put away neatly in my drawers. I studied myself in the mirror making faces of annoyance at myself, my spiky hair was still standing even though I'd been asleep for hours, my eyes were barely open, I staggered; groaning like a zombie to the bathroom and leaned supporting myself over the sink then splashed handfuls of icy cool water onto my face in some desperate attempt to wake myself. My eyelids flipped open immediately and a quick shiver shot through my spine, well that worked! Maybe soon I'll find another less wet way of achieving that in the early mornings. So now it was time for another boring day in the life of Lee.

I ran downstairs, noticing no one was in as usual and put the kettle on , then roamed around the kitchen in search of food. A bag of crisps for breakfast, my everyday choice. The kettle boiled and the button flipped off then I poured the steaming, hot water into my mug. The morning went on as normal, a crappy array of eating, watching TV, wandering about needlessly then, to break the monotony, there was a knock at the door, they hammered through the air three times. I thought nothing of it, probably just my mum returning, oh boy… I walked slowly to the door, no need to rush, never any need to rush, eyeing the tall black shadow: not my mum; she was very short. Torn bits of cloth waved in the cold, wintry breeze around its clothes. I frowned, who could it be? I started rushing, forgetting the fact that I was only wearing a jumper and boxer shorts. I swung the door open then gasped aloud as I saw there was no-one there!! I checked the steps then stumbled down the garden path opening my front gate which screeched like a dying bat, immediately I noticed how everything seemed to be weird about the street, something was out of place but… what? Something was different but… what? It was as though the air was strangled by some kind of evil presence, I stared down the deserted roads. Nowhere for someone to hide and no-one could have run and gotten away down this long stretch of straight road, freaky!!!

So I went back inside, quickly forgetting all about it, brushing the thoughts away and returning right back to normal life, shutting the door briskly behind me. I made my way up the stairs and took a shower, the scorching hot sprays of water revitalizing me, ready for the rest of the day ahead. I re-gelled my hair, spiking it up into a tall, black flame, my usual style. What to do for the whole day now? I wandered the house for ages aimlessly… again, waiting for an idea to pop into my head. Soooo bored, no school for that day, it was Saturday and the middle of the summer holidays anyway, not that I was disappointed that I wasn't going to school, that was a drag too.

I threw myself onto the sofa and flipped franticly through the channels on TV. News rubbish, children's programs, daytime TV, Loose women, Jeremy Kyle??? Why in the world was I wasting my time?? I heard the kettle click off, signaling that it had finished its boil, but… wait, was I going crazy? I didn't turn it on! Did I? I had only just had my last cup, right? I raced to the kitchen passing a random pile of old, unread magazines. I entered through the door way of my kitchen and spotted the kettle on the side, staying still not moving, doing what it normally did… nothing. Well, what did I expect it to do? Jump up and start doing the Can-Can?! Then, to my surprise the red light which signaled it was boiling switched on all by itself, then flickered off, then on, then off, growing rapidly in pace for every second it did it. I stared dumbly watching the kettle turn off then on. Then when it reached an impossible pace and couldn't go any faster it just stopped! Dead! Did I imagine it? I couldn't have, could I? Maybe if it happened just the once, maybe my mind could have been playing tricks but all those times? It couldn't have just been me seeing things. But what happened next answered my question, the kitchen light flickered on, lighting the otherwise dark and gloomy room; I looked up in disbelief, this light too? How could this be happening?! The next second it exploded, the glass falling and showering my face with hundreds of sharp, tiny splinters.

Chapter two: The chase

It had been a whole week since that freaky... well whatever it was happened, I told my mum all about it but she just said 'The light broke' WHAT!!? I bloody knew better than that! My friend Raze who lived a few doors down from me said it was a ghost, I didn't believe in ghosts, that idea was stupid. But then again, I couldn't explain it so it could have been, I guess... Just then somebody knocked at the door, three long ear-ringing echoes bounced through the house; I shuddered. Mum hadn't been in all morning so it was just like last time, me alone, no-one else to witness the disappearance, same day of the week, Saturday, no cars on the ghost roads. The door didn't knock again, any normal person would have knocked continuously to make sure the person inside heard, but with this guy, it seemed as though he knew I was in! I slowly walked towards the door, taking small steps, my breathing growing ragged and sharp. That time I was wearing trousers and trainers ready to make a run after the person if I had to, I was prepared! It was the same shadow, just like before, strips of cloth waved in the wind but I noticed something I hadn't before, there *was* no wind: the well-tempered weeks of summer had remained true and the weather had been calm and hot for days on end now. I stepped past the pile of unread magazines when something caught my eye ...on the cover of the magazine! I turned and stared at it, I began to think it was only my eyes playing tricks on me when I saw it again, the picture of the woman on the cover moved!!! She shouted words that I couldn't hear, waving her hands above her head then she pointed at the door and turned red before falling still again. I blinked, I didn't imagine that I couldn't have and THAT definitely wasn't a ghost! I shook my head in disbelief but moved on knowing that I had to focus on the man at the door, I opened it, no one there, that was it!

I ran to the bottom of my path, opening the gate I quickly checked behind the bushes. Nothing! This was crazy!! Then, out of the corner of my eye, I saw something move down the bottom of the otherwise empty road, I turn my head swiftly catching a glimpse of a black piece of material. I chased it without hesitation, when I reached the end of the road I stopped, eyeing the next street for movement. A couple of lonely shop-keepers remained, groaning over their pain of selling nothing as usual. I frowned, this was crazy, how could someone run that fast or just disappear!!? It was impossible! My eyes scanned the street, past the desolate shops and stopped at the corner, another glimpse of black clothing, behind a green recycling bin. I caught up with it and spun to where I saw it but once again it was gone! My eyes darted everywhere; I spotted it again now wondering if I was just seeing things, how else could you explain the disappearances? A long black cape that automatically had my mind screaming VAMPIRE! draped over a shadowy figure, that time it was on top of one of the corner shops roofs, but it had stopped now, I stepped closer looking for anything that would give me a clue as to who the mysterious figure was; I saw nothing! Just a gothic styled cape hanging in mid-air, the torn strips of cloth at the ends reaching

11

the floor, brushing the dust along the ground. From where I was it looked like it had no feet, but that was easily explained as the torn material at the ends could have been covering them up, the thing that was more confusing was the fact that I couldn't see its head; it must have been a person but where the hell was its head? Was it a hunchback or something? I reached the shop and search the wall looking for something to climb without even thinking how mad that sounded; the shop-keeper wasn't looking so I started my ascent. I scaled the wall clinging on to an unusually strong drain pipe; it was a miracle that I didn't fall off.

My hands finally reached the top and grabbed tightly around the edges of brick work, pulling up my weight. I forced myself onto the ledge and got to my feet focusing on the floating cape. Approaching it cautiously I circled it, gasping in amazement as I saw that there was nothing on the other side, no-one holding it up, nothing holding it up! It took me a while to even notice the cape was starting to glow red slowly and gradually from a dim light to a powerful burst of almost blinding light, the light rays formed impossibly into what I recognized as a dragons head, without warning it shot forward head butting me hard in the stomach, I looked down, my jaw dropping comically, it had bitten right through me! There was a huge gapping hole in my chest! I exhaled white smoke and my eyes rolled back, I fell backwards, everything went blank.

Chapter three: Death threats

My eyes flipped open instinctively gasping for life. Darkness, the floor was stone cold against my back. I was looking up into the night sky dotted with several gleaming stars. The cape was gone, the light was out, no dragon to be seen. I could barely even remember what had happened. I got up after a few minutes of disorientated half consciousness, then brushing myself off dizzily, holding my head, tried to make sense out of what had happened; what the hell was that light? Eventually after getting no further with my investigation and recovering from my intense head ache I jumped down the building landing half way on the ledge before stepping down onto the ground level. I pushed my tangled perplexed thoughts aside and staggered home like a lost drunk.

Mum was already there but she had gone to bed, it was about ten. The front door was shut but I managed to slip in using the secret key under the stone next to the door step. I crept to bed without waking my mum and pulled over the covers wrapping myself up in a defensive ball before eagerly falling asleep once again.

I was walking through my house in almost complete darkness. Looking for something to do as usual, I was bored to death. I didn't think about turning on any lights, I guess I didn't want to wake my mum. The door knocked, then stopped. The shadow appeared at the glass. This time it was reaching for me, stretching a hand towards the glass, the strips of black material blowing around viciously a lot more than before. I reached the door handle unsure then prepared to turn it when the glass smashed, specks of it cutting across my back. I yelled as a hand grabbed me by the scruff of my neck

"You shouldn't keep me waiting, you should rush to me, do nothing to anger me. But you are beyond saving now, I am an impatient person, you knew I was knocking for you and you still took your time! The next time I knock you should run, run for your life, because I will not leave you in peace any more, the next time…you die!"

The voice was of a man and oddly didn't sound at all like an angry, evil, hiss but a soft, gentle, solemn tone, which made it even worse, even more creepy! I screamed as I was thrown back down the hallway. Before I knew it I was staring up in terror at a pale faced, tall, black clad man. He had black lips and dark shapes around his eyes, like eyeliner used as paint, the bottom halves drawn into three curved triangles his eyes were overrun by bloodshot veins, his hair was spiked up much taller than mine, it was black but with an unnerving, blood red tint to it. His face had a massive cut taken out of it, down the left side, I could see his cheek bone through it! He wore an immaculate black suit with a simple red tie. He smiled thinly, his black lips stretching and revealing the bloody cracks dotted around on them, he then tapped my forehead with one bony finger, the nail looked like it hadn't been cut in months and sliced a line out of my skin. He showed his teeth; I couldn't help but gasp, they were sharp like a shark's and had chunks of meat slotted in many places. My voice came from out of no-where,

"Are you a vampire?" I trembled.

"No" he chuckled darkly. "Although, I know some… No, child, I am your worst nightmare". At that he clapped his hands and pulled his top set of teeth over his bottom lip and bit, blood erupting and flooding down his chin. He opened his mouth and let it fill with a pool of blood then said, spilling the blood freely, "Wakey, wakey".

Chapter four: The escape

I woke screaming, shaking viciously my entire body on fire. Someone barged in slamming the door against my wall, my head whipped around and I started to yell, it was another monster.

"No! Get away!! Leave me alone!! Leave me!!" I roared in terror. Its face turned to a mask of confused concern.

"What's wrong?" She shrieked stepping towards me, I abruptly slid back in my bed until I was pressed tight against the wall screaming so loud my vocal cords would burst but when the creature reached the edge of my bed I realized I was confused, her face slowly molded into that of my mother's.

"What's wrong?" she repeated.

"The monster!" I screamed.

"What monster?!"

"He said he would kill me!" I roared.

"You were only dreaming, it was only a nightmare" she explained. I shook my head of all those terrible memories and began to protest but then realized she was right, my shoulders sagged, my whole body drooping, every muscle suddenly relaxing as one.

"I know" I sighed at being soooo stupid, I was such an idiot!

"Sorry. It was just so real".

She shook her head. "Silly. And how did you get that cut? You must have hit your head in your sleep, oh you –"

"What?!" I cut her off.

"The cut, its all the way across your forehead" She said wiping it with

16

her sleeve.

"WHAT!? WHAT!? WHAT?! THE MAN! The dream was real!!

"He cut me! His nails, like claws, a monster, teeth, sharp teeth, vampires!!"

Babbling incoherently now, my mind was giving way to madness.

"He said he would knock! He said the next time!! He will come and kill me!"

My mum's face was caked in fear for me. I grabbed my mum and pulled closer staring into her eyes, mine filled with terror.

"We've got to leave!! NOW!"

Later on I calmed down clutching a hot chocolate in my hands, still trembling slightly unable to completely shake off the memory. I explained the apparent nightmare and how I knew it was real. That I had seen the shadow outside of the door before, I gave a thorough description of the man. She didn't believe me of course but eventually, after a long stressful amount of time she began to accept that I would not calm down fully unless we moved houses, went somewhere else completely, far away! She told me that the house would be a lot smaller and not nearly as good, probably a flat; it seemed like she was trying to change my mind but I didn't care what the new house was like as long as it was far away from there so the monster couldn't get me. So finally after many days of arguments we packed our bags and left... While we were in the car, I saw signs moving as if by magic, a billboard with a pack of cigarettes display jumped along it about a meter following after me, the cigarette packet caught alight and the flames engulfed the whole board. I pointed it out to my mum but she couldn't seem to see what I could. The flames formed into letters that spelt 'You can run, but you can't hide' and then a cartoon cigarette appeared and laughed at me, manically pointing evilly after me down the road. I shuddered. I knew then. It wasn't the end...

Chapter five: Back to normal

It had been a month since. Everything was fine - well, kind of. I still had nightmares but I had no more injuries from them. So all it turned into was my worst nightmare ever! The memory of it always so fresh in my mind, I wondered sometimes how I got that cut, if it was a dream then how could the wound be real? Dreams don't work like that. But it obviously was a dream right? I didn't know if the monster from the dream was real but if it wasn't then it seemed so realistic. The house I was staying in now was actually a house, not a flat. But it might as well have been because it only had one room up stairs, my mum's room. My bedroom was downstairs, a small room, one chest of drawers, one single bed, that's it. I kept my books and other possessions under my bed so I had a small bit of room next to it to write books and read or whatever. Outside there are loads of amusement arcades so I played there a lot of the time. I had nightmares of the arcades exploding and collapsing on me but that didn't put me off. I knew that there just nightmares and nothing else, they couldn't hurt me. I could control myself and forget about my nightmares so they couldn't interfere with my life, I mean, I would be a total wreck otherwise. Everything was back to normal, back to humanity, no more monsters.

I was in my house finishing off a reading book, I was right near the end, on the chapter where you find out who the thief was, the big finale when, knocking. Three knocks, then they stopped. I felt a familiar shudder race up my spine, my heart sunk, and I cautiously got up from my book and opened my bedroom door not shutting it after me, I wanted some where to run for when the monster chased me. I stepped into the hallway turning my head slowly, carefully towards the front door.

The shadow was there in the glass window of the door. The same as always, black clothes, stripes of material hanging off, this time they were not blowing, maybe because this time they were different, this time he wanted to kill me unlike the other times, that's what he said wasn't it? I reached slowly for the door my hand grasping the handle it slipping from the intense sweat on my palms. Then I quickly swung it open, a scream bubbling up in my throat … I relaxed. It was only an old lady! Dressed in a black coat with a torn up shopping bag in her hand. She smiled warmly.

"I'm not that scary am I?" she laughed.

"Oh …no, sorry, I was expecting someone else" I answered taking a shaky breath of relief in.

"Can I help you?" I added.

"No! I can help you" There was a couple of seconds silence then she showed me the bag.

"I bring sweeties!" She was old but how young did she think I was?!

"Oh thanks" I replied awkwardly as she handed me the bag full of chocolate.

"No need to thank me" she chuckled "You've just moved in and I have money spare so I will bring you food and snacks to keep us the best of neighbours… if that's okay?"

"Thank you" I nodded politely, she then moved off down the four steps and down the road. I had got to stop being so scared of the door being knocked because generally a lot in normal life.

Chapter six: New friends

The old lady, Miss Cook, brought us food every now and then:
chocolate and baked food like cakes, bread and biscuits. She was
quite friendly but weird and made me feel like a two year old but it
was always good having an old lady bringing you cooked food for all
the times when my mum couldn't be bothered to make any thing
herself which was a lot of the time. Not long ago my mum was
always around, always in the house. I didn't have to fend for myself
so much, I'd always be sure of getting a cooked dinner from her but
now she was out pretty much once everyday at least, I guess she
just thought I was old enough to look after myself, I didn't care, I **was**
thirteen after all. Life was good and I didn't think it would change.
Then again my life would have gotten boring if it stayed the same I
guess. I was on my way to the arcades like I did most days, there
was nothing really to do at home anymore, no new TV shows, I'd
finished my reading book and my writing was stuck on a huge writers
block. Everything was boring again like I said it would be.

 I always had loads of money when I went to the arcades. Walking
past cramped shops that were very much open unlike my old area, I
reached my arcade heaven and fished out my money from my
pockets, rushing for my favourite game. I didn't know the name
because the sign saying what it was called was worn away: the
arcades were ancient. The game was one of the shoot 'em-ups, I
had completed it so many times I was the master of it! When I got

there though, I saw to my despair that some one else was in my place already playing on it! How dare they!? I groaned then stood next to it, watching. The intruder was a girl with long red hair and she was wearing a cowboy's hat, a white top cut off at the sleeves and a pair of jeans. She was about my age and getting really far on the game. I watched her character getting killed, she then groaned, stopped and turned to me.

"Do you wanna play?" she asked kindly "Two player?" My eyes brightened, I nodded happily.

"Well all you needed to do was ask" She said pulling out a pound coin to insert into the machine.

"No!" I yelled as she froze.

"What?!"

"I'll pay for you" I said calming down with the volume

"Nah, you don't have to" She said brushing it off

"No, it would be my pleasure" I smiled, I don't know why I did that... I acted like an idiot! But luckily she returned the smile.

" Ok, thanks" She shrugged, I put in two coins and we started the game. We spent ages killing people together, she was good! I had been killed twice and she had only just lost one life! I thought I was the master! I didn't mind though she didn't gloat or anything like anyone else would have. Her name was Roxy. We shot until I run out of money

"Damn!" I shouted dropping my guns. "No more money"

"Ohhh that's ok, hey..." She trailed off looking at her feet then continued "Can I come to your house?" Roxy asked.

I couldn't stop a grin of victory creeping across my face "Errrrr, yeah, I think. That would be cool"

"Yay!!" She said then smiled then that was it! We walked off together into the sunset. I thought I was so cool, I had got myself a girlfriend!!! HELL YEAH!!!

Chapter seven: Anybody home?

I was at home, Roxy had gone, I could relax again. I was in the best of moods, I'd got a girlfriend! I hadn't had one before so I was also a bit scared and nervous, but I thought everything would go well. She was well cool! She loved computer games, definitely shooting ones (**My** favourite) she was a lot more skilled than me but that was wicked, It was so great. Mum was out as usual, to the shops I thought. I was on my own, I thought about calling Roxy, I knew she had just been round but she was kind of taking over my life. I got up to go and dial her number when the door knocked, she was there already!! She must be missing me THAT much! I rushed excitedly into the hall way and stopped dead, fear struck me like a freight train, I was being stupid it was only Miss Cook with her trademark ripped shopping bags. I started towards the door again and opened it expecting the old lady to be there waiting to give me her food. I screamed in shock, my whole body breaking out in uncontrollable shakes of terror.

"Oh no! Not you!"

It was not Miss Cook, it was not Roxy, it was not any of my friends at all. In fact the total opposite, my worst nightmare! Like before he was tall, pale-faced and deathly menacing but instead of his suit he was wearing a long black cape which was wrapped around his waist and a black shirt, the same red tie as before. He floated forward grinning with his vampire-like teeth.

"Let uncle Darkne in, Lee" he whispered. "You wouldn't want to anger me would you?!" He said his last words in a hiss. I screeched at him edging away, backwards down the hall, I could feel my muscles losing power, my body shutting down, my world going to hell.

"Don't run, small child!" He snarled. "I don't wish to hurt you. Only to kill you" His voice returned to the hushed, solemn tone.
"You're real?!" I gasped "Not just a dream?!"
"No, no, no, no, no Lee. Not just a dream, I'm one hundred per cent real. And your death will be one hundred per cent real, right now!" Something within me clicked and I rushed forward bashing into the monster, pushing him out of the door with all my might. I slammed the door right on his face and fell back on the door mat, crazy adrenaline pumping through my veins, it was far from over though. His hand snaked through the letter box grabbing for me. I kicked at it, his voice sounded.
"Do you ever wonder how I can hurt you in your dreams, or how I can float or how I can explode lights and ruin kettles?" He asked.
"How?" My voice squeaked from the fear constricting my throat.
"Because I'm not human...I am a magic man!" With that his hand slid back through the letter box and the house began to shake viciously as if there was an earthquake. The pictures on the wall fell to the floor and smashed around me. I dropped straight to my belly, flattening myself to the floor crawling through the madness, glass slitting my skin like needles; I was trying to make it to the bathroom. I got to my feet and jumped through the door shutting it behind me.

"You don't have a clue what you're up against" He roared, shaking the house even more. His voice sounding amplified. The taps erupted and the water shot out like fountains. Covering me.

"Ok!" He shouted. Everything stopped immediately "That's it, I will leave you alone for now but if you tell anyone about me I'll come back and your death will come sooner then originally planned. Goodbye child" …Silence. Just like that the taps mended, the water evaporated and the pictures flew back onto the walls the glass gluing itself back together as though nothing had happened, no evidence at all as to what happened. Impossible! It was crazy! Too crazy!!

Chapter eight: Lies

I was sitting in the middle of the front room when my mum came in. It had been two days since the last visit from 'Uncle Darkne' as he called himself: his sick sense of humour I suppose. I thought after that that he was actually human, not a monster at all.

But if he was, he was a mad man with a great amount of some kind of magical, out of this world power. He said he could use magic! He also said as I remember 'If you tell anyone about me I'll come back and kill you.' That sent a shiver down my spine. So he was still going to kill me and I couldn't tell anyone or else he'd kill me sooner. I was trapped!

"Your nightmares have gotten worse lately" My mum noted.

Yes!! That's because I knew a madman was after me and would kill me any second! I couldn't tell her though, not ever, I had to keep quiet.

"Yeah, but not about the monster" I lied. She frowned and sat down with me on the carpet.

"So, now you're having nightmares about something else as well?"

"No, not as well, the ones about the monster have gone now, they went ages ago, now it's just these new ones" I was doing ok so far.

"Any idea why these new nightmares have come?" She asked

"No"

"Would you like to tell me what they are about?"

"No"

"Ok then, if that's how you want to be. I've called a psychotherapist for you, he can help you" She explained.

"What?!" I exploded "No!"

"He can stop your nightmares" she insisted. I went to argue my point but stopped myself; I thought that if I put up too much of a fight she would have suspected something. But I then had to deal with a professional! Damn parents. If only there was a way she could have found out without me having to tell her then she might have helped me out of the situation I'm now in. Too bad!

The man arrived soon after. My mum had called him long before our chat and he came straight away. We sat in the kitchen, mum was asked to leave the room. I and the psychotherapist sat on opposite sides of the kitchen table on wooden seats. He sat eyeing me for a few seconds. I knew I'd have to lie my way out of the tricky situation, but it wasn't going to be easy.

"So, your nightmares of this... creature have stopped?" He asked starting the session.

"Yes, totally, no more creature" I smiled falsely at him.

"Ok but am I correct in thinking different nightmares have started?"

"Yes but there not as bad" I answered, once again lying.

"Remember, you must tell me the truth about everything... ok?"

I had a sudden, strong, uncontainable urge to just burst out with the truth right there and then, tell him that a madman had threatened me with death. But he wouldn't have believed me or not straight away at least and by the time he did I knew it would be too late.

"Do you think that maybe ...those old nightmares have taken on a new form in these new nightmares?" He questioned.

"No way! If they had then they would be as scary as the old ones, these new nightmares aren't as bad, not by a long shot"

"Ok" He said, about to quiz me even more. But he couldn't help me, no one could!!

Chapter nine: Blood on my hands

The psychotherapist left soon after and so did mum, going out again, I didn't know where to and like usual she didn't tell me. I tried to make her stay, I begged her, I said that I wanted to talk to her about my nightmares. She just replied

"You should have told that man everything, now you've missed your chance" If only she knew. I fort and fort but she simply left. Running out of ideas I grabbed the phone and called Roxy. I didn't think Darkne would attack me if someone else was in the house, if there was someone else to witness the destruction, I just prayed to god that she was in. My heart stopped, she was! She picked up the phone.

"Yes!" I shouted

"Hello?" She replied surprised

"Can you come round?" I asked quickly, not wanting to get into a full blown conversation.

"Err, yeah ok, I'll be round in-"

"Yeah ok, great, goodbye" I cut in, hanging up. I sighed with relief. I then waited for her to arrive, impatient, thinking about would happen if Darkne attacked while she was on her way. Actually ...why didn't he? I tried to calm myself down and relax for another ten minutes but the fear kept a constant pace, I jumped at every small sound, teeth chattering like the tapping of a computer keyboard.

The door knocked and I almost died from shock. It was her! I was safe! I smiled dropping all my anxiety, it felt soooo good. I opened the door to her, my smile beaming.

"You look happy, but you sounded a bit …err…crazy on the phone. Is everything alright between us?" She said. My smile shook, I was about to tell her everything, I had to stop myself; with a huge deal of courage I held the secret back.

"Yes everything is alright, why wouldn't it be?" I asked.

"Oh, ok, well your just a bit jumpy" She replied.

"No! Not at all!" I snapped. She looked hurt, but I couldn't comfort her at that moment in time, my fear had reformed

"Errrrr, ok, would you like to read my gaming comics with me?" I asked, that would break the tension… hopefully.

"Yeah, of course" She answered. So at that we went to my room and got out some old game comics and started to read them out.

I was just about to read out an article on the latest game of that time when the writing changed print.

"No!" I roared kicking the comic to one side, my body juddering uncontrollably. Roxy looked up in jaw dropping confusion.

"What the hell is wrong with you?"

"Look!" I shouted, my lips trembling, I went to grab the book then showed her the words 'I'm coming to get you' It read.

"What? What's so weird about seven out of ten?" She asked, her forehead creasing her eyes full of frightened concern

"No! Can't you see?!" I cried with desperation.

"No, obviously I can't"

I lost it then ripped the book to pieces, tearing it to shreds like a rabid wolf.

"Calm down!" Her eyes were wide with terror, I bit into my fingers madly, Stricken with fear.

"He's coming, he's gonna kill me!" I shuddered

"What?! Who is?"

"He's a murderer!" I screamed.

"Who?"

"He's Thomas Darkne, he said he would kill me!"

"Don't be stupid" she trembled. The door knocked like the ringing of a knell right on queue.

"No!!! It's HIM!" I shrieked. Roxy got up and left the room shaking her head with disbelief, going to open the door.

"NO! Don't open the door!" I warned chasing her down the hall, my legs pumping like mental

"For god's sake! It isn't a murderer, that's only in your nightmares" She answered ignoring my pleas, disappointed.

"No!!!!!!!!" I yelled rushing down the corridor snatching up an oddly placed object from the floor. I caught up with her and blindly drove the metal through her back before her fingers closed around the door knob. She fell to the ground going limp; I caught her in my arms. I cried in shock, staring down at my kill, my heart thudding against my chest so loud all other sounds were drowned out. What had I become?! I watched down in horror at the deep, ruby red blood on my hands!!

Chapter ten: Chat with Darkne.

My tears rolled down my face and dropped off onto Roxy splashing upon her cold dead face. Her blood trickled off my hands and onto the wooden floorboards, drenching them. I couldn't believe it! I had killed her!! Her eyes were frozen, there's no forgetting someone's round, lifeless, dead eyes. In a flash the front door exploded, splinters hit me all over showering me with wood. Darkne stepped through the broken door frame, no one had to open it for him now, he picked Roxy off the floor using magic, his hands by his sides. "Hello, Lee. This is your pathetic girlfriend?" A grin slowly formed on his wicked face and then he clicked his fingers, she exploded! Her flesh bounced off of the walls smearing them in blood, the thick meaty chunks hit the floor and separated into even smaller, bloodier segments before melting directly through the wood. I looked up, totally destroyed, inside and out. The maniac was holding Roxy's arms and legs, the only remaining pieces of her, he fixed them together, each leg to an arm and danced them around in front of me like some demented, demonic puppet.
"Do you wanna play?" He asked, really enjoying this. "Two player?"

His eyes dropped to me looking sad.
 "Poor Lee, poorly" He laughed in a deep cackle. "Get it?
Poor...Lee?"
I spat at his feet, he frowned.
"Why?" He whispered, he looked hurt "We could be such good

friends. You're already half crazy and I'm, erm… different. We could rule this universe together, father and…no. You don't have the taste for human flesh, unlike me" His eye lit up then he bit into Roxy's severed arm, blood spurting over his face, he smiled open-mouthed, bits of flesh logged in his teeth.

"Please, kill me now" I murmured

"Erm… no" He answered.

"WHAT?!" I yelled "You said, you said… You'd kill me!" I whimpered not even feeling anything for hearing that.

"Oh sorry, you may have mistaken my meaning, your spirit is well and truly slaughtered is it not? I never planned to kill you, not even at the start. It will be much better for me to let you live a life of craziness, and pain, I could watch you go insane, wouldn't take too long." He explained

"No! You're lying, you are going to kill me" I screamed.

"No!" He hissed "Did you ever wonder why your mum was never in the house when I visited?" He asked, seeming to be growing impatient.

"You waited for her to leave" I shouted

"No, no, no, no, I told her to leave"

"What?! Why would she listen to you?"

"She had no choice; I controlled her sweet little brain. I made her think up the idea of leaving. Do you remember when your mother agreed to moving house?"

"Of course I do!"

"Didn't you stop and think, why did she agree so quickly without too much of a fight?" There was a long pause then he started again.

"That was me too, I told her to leave"

"WHY?!"I roared

"I like to toy with my victims you see, I like to fill them with hope of escape only to strike them down at the last second. I made Roxy meet you at the arcades; I placed the knife on the hall way floor. I set this whole thing up like a scene from a tragic play"

"NO!!" I roared.

His smile widened. "I filled your life with people that I could just kill off for the extra pleasure; all they were were meat puppets. But it's not all bad" He paused "I've got you a present. I hope you like". I began to crawl away but he stopped me.

"Don't move...My present" He reminded me sticking me to the floor using purple webs, I couldn't even struggle.

He clicked his fingers and a round white ball appeared in his hand. He rolled it to me like a bowling ball and as it got closer I realized, it was my mum's head! The meat of half of the neck was all chopped and torn away. My eyes widened, my brain swelling with unstoppable insanity, my mind clouding over, my soul slipping away, the last words I hear him say before I lose control altogether are...

"Remember my name: THO...MAS...DARK...NE, Your life long tormenter!"

THE END

Torture two: Mass-occurring mayhem

In this part you will be shown the first small insight to Darkne's ultimate magical potential as he unleashes it on a young man called Danny, but has he messed with the wrong guy?

Chapter one: Let chaos commence

I have experienced many weird things in my life, that's what inspired me to write this novel based on my life. It wasn't so long ago when it first started. I'm not great at writing but I don't have to be because all this is one hundred per cent real, should be pretty easy to simply write it all out from memory. It first started when I was making tea, I can't remember what day or any tiny insignificant details like that but I could remember the kettle had just boiled when I was crossing the hallway, I heard something outside smash, like a glass jar or something, it seemed to have come from the alleyway which ran along side my flat. It was where we kept our rubbish bins piled in. It obviously wasn't that amazing, a jar smashing big deal! But then a second smash, sounding like a twin of the last one. I finally decided to investigate and strolled over to my window which over looked the alley. Leaning out over the window seal, I could see the green wheelie bins outside and a cardboard box lying across them side ways like a shooting range, ten jars where lined up along it. I frowned, scanning the alley for life. No cats or dogs or foxes that could have knocked them over, I could see no one else down there. Nothing! Then just as I was about to give up and go back inside to collect my tea another jar exploded right before my eyes!! I blinked, amazed, rubbing my eyes in disbelieve but all the evidence was there, I could see the small specks of glass that lay around. Impossible! Another one smashed. I decided I had to see this close up so without wasting any time I ran to my door and swung on my denim jacket from the coat rack knocking it to the floor in my excitement.

I rushed down the stairs of the flat and blasted out the front door, turning down the alleyway. I was close enough to read the labels on the jars now when another one fell apart. My eyes darted to the windows of the surrounding flats; each of which were mysteriously empty, then I looked to the street behind me. No one was there! I couldn't see anyone, as far as I could see I was alone. I turned slowly back round to the jars as they smashed one by one, me jumping back to dodge the sparks of glass. Then the collections of jars were totally destroyed: it seemed almost as if some invisible person was holding an invisible gun firing invisible bullets at them in turn. I spun around again just to be safe but I was sure there was no one there. Why would anyone be hiding? And if someone was hiding ... where? There was no where to hide. Something bounced off the bin lid behind me and pinged off of the walls ricocheting everywhere.

I ducked instinctively, burying my head in my arms in defence. More invisible bullets pinned into the bins, when I felt like I could risk a sneak peek I looked up and spotted three bullet shaped holes indented in the green plastic material, what was happening? How could this be real? Not needing to be hanging around I jumped up and dived for the cover of the wheelie bin, hiding behind it. I poked my head around the side; no one was there, still a mystery. I got back behind cover just in time for more bullets to clink off the walls. They repeated fire for ages so I waited for them to stop, covering my face with my arms in case of a stray bullet hitting me in the head, not daring to move and peek around the corner again.

Finally after what seemed like hours the firing had stopped so I stepped out from cover and walked cautiously very very cautiously down the alley, expecting the gun to shoot again and for the unseen bullets to cut me down. They didn't and I safely escaped the alley of death letting out a breath of relief. The posh lady from the next block of flats opened her window slightly then thrust her scrawny head out, she shouted down at me,
"What in the world was that racket Daniel?!"
My name's Danny, lady, get it right. I looked up and replied in the most sincere but snob like voice I could muster,
"I don't have a clue actually, awfully sorry that I ruined your lovely, charming, peaceful day of luxury" Then I whispered below my breath "Witch". I returned to my flat soon after. But I really didn't know what that was all about, just a complete mystery.

Chapter two: Bring on the mysteries

The next time, weird happening number two, I was at work, Comet, you know, the best place in the world to work, oh yeah shop at Comet! Anyway...I had to work at the tills on that day; not my usual job, I had talked to old men who wanted to buy wind up radios and wooden TV's. I had to explain why we didn't have any, a very difficult task as It meant me repeating myself ten times for each sentence, explaining the same things over and over again hoping that a miracle would happen and they'd get it into their heads. One gave up and just asked where the toilet was I had to take him to it otherwise I'm sure he would have done it where he stood, not the best thing in the world then your trying to sell stuff to customers. Luckily they left eventually.

Soon after a rush of people who actually knew what they were doing I was left alone behind the counter watching the large wide screen televisions flick through adverts. Something about cat food was on when it happened. The TV went off, dead! I groaned and walked around the till to find out what the problem was. I reached it and was about to give fixing it a go when the screen flashed on again. I jumped backwards in shock. What happened there? The cat food advert had finished and another started; a black background then a floating red tie, it circled the screen three times then stopped, hanging in mid air in the centre, I frowned, I'd never seen that advert before. It looked freaky and surreal from the start, a man dressed in a black suit appeared as the black background melted into red. He had long, spiked, black hair, a pale face with a huge, long slice taken out of the left side, he had blood down his suit like trickles of fresh red paint and drool running down his chin. His lips were black and he was wearing a hell of a lot of eyeliner in some weird modern twist on Egyptian style. He opened his mouth to speak showing a long, cut up, snake-like tongue, badly chapped lips and a set of very sharp looking teeth. He talked in a low, solemn tone.

"Hello pathetic humans" he greeted softly. "My name is Thomas Darkne, I can't say it's a pleasure to meet you, but soon you will all be dead so it won't matter to me. There is no stopping Thomas Darkne, once he has chosen you, you must kneel to your fate, a long painful death. The human race is weak and ready to be crushed. I will be the dealer of death" My eyes widened, was he speaking to us?

"Good night and remember to prepare for the dawn of death"

Then letters appeared on the screen "The wrath of Thomas Darkne" And I noticed it was only a film trailer, how stupid was I? The man's face flickered back on the TV screen, he smiled like a shark before disappearing into a black background. Words stamped onto the screen. 'In cinemas August the eighth' I stopped, I tutted, those kind of adverts shouldn't have been on that early, it would scare kids to death, I thought, it gave me enough of a fright.

Without warning a TV ripped off of its stand and fired itself towards me. I spotted it at the last second and jumped to the side making it collide with the wall behind me, the others followed it aiming at me. My eyes bulged and I dropped to the floor, the TV's joining their destroyed comrade on the counter, smashed to bits. I turned then with nothing else to say shouted, "Damn!!"

Chapter three: Magic man

I spent the next three days off work; they thought I was crazy and that I had smashed the TV's in a sudden burst of madness! ME?! Crazy?! They didn't fire me because I was such a great worker, with my incredible powers I could deal with even the most senile old men when they walked in, without a clue as to why they were there. But I wasn't crazy, I was being attacked by televisions and invisible guns, was that so hard to believe? Obviously it was… It was time to get some help. Later I wrote letters on websites about what was happening, most of the replies were from psychotherapist saying I was being disturbed by something, others were from mentalists, endless emails from people with obvious mental problems, but then one of the replies was different, stood out from the rest of the crazy jumble, from a man who seemed to know what he was talking about and what I was talking about. He sounded a bit strange but not crazy, talking about dark forces. He said for me to go to his place, he left his address on the email. I left it for a while longer and tried other people trying to see if I could get any closer to an answer but soon it became all too obvious that no one could help except maybe, hopefully, the strange, dark forces guy.

The address led me to the middle of nowhere, I had gone by train, then by bus, then finished off by walking. It was a small village, more like a single road. No one around: the place was empty apart from three aligned houses, the road looked deserted. The houses were numbered 1 to 4 missing out 3. There was a gap where it would have been, and that was exactly where the guy was supposed to live. I thought he was strange… His house didn't even exist!

I gave a long, annoyed, disappointed sigh then as I was about to leave I heard the abrupt screeching of car wheels. I span around spotting a black camper van grind to a halt, a few seconds later and the door opened, a bulky man with huge broad shoulders like an ox stepped out and frowned at me from under his long brown scruffy hair.

"Ah, yes, Danny" He said shutting the door

"Hello, erm, Glad…I'm….here"

"Gladimere" He corrected me. "It's pronounced Glad-dim-ear"

I nodded awkwardly and he looked at the camper, tutting. "I've always wanted one with flames sprayed up the sides, will have soon though I bet" With that he walked past me towards the gap in the short row of houses.

"Erm, your house?" I asked, not sure if I should just leave the obviously insane old guy to it.

"Oh yes, of course" He paused "This will be a bit shocking for you I suppose so prepare yourself" He said clicking his fingers, I watched in amazement as the gap started to fill itself in with bricks forming into a house with windows, doors and everything! I gasped almost losing my footing, not fully believing my eyes, had I lost it too?

"Told you" He chuckled, walking through the door casually. I quickly stepped through after him before my legs gave way, lights flickered on around me.

Gladimere was sitting on the sofa smiling.

"Confusing isn't it?" He laughed "But I am here to tell you everything. I am a magic man as an old friend of mine would say " He said. I sat down next to him on the sofa shaking slightly.

"What? Magic? As in spells and stuff?" I asked trying to sound calm when really I was preparing to escape if necessary.

"Yes exactly. I will make this meeting as short as possible... This invisible force is a magic being like me" He explained

"Ok... but I think it wants to kill me" I said nodding concerned.

"Yes" He agrees. "This one is very dangerous, it is trying to kill you, its an evil magician called Thomas Darkne, he uses magic to torture people" He said his next words slowly. "He has chosen you"

"WHAT?!" I shouted "He wants to torture me?!"

"Yes and you will die unless you fight back. Have you seen him before?" He asked.

"No, he has attacked me with invisible bullets and thrown teles at me," I explained

"Ah, yes, finger trigger" He nodded.

"What?"

"Nothing" He scoffed "but normally he lets his victims see him, by dream or electrical devices or anything of the sort... Are you sure you haven't seen him?"

"No, I haven't seen him." Then it all fell into place. "Wait! Thomas Darkne! Yes, he was on a film trailer!!" I gasped remembering the freaky looking man. "The wrath of Thomas Darkne" I added "Yes, you are in deep trouble" Gladimere said grimly.

Chapter four: In-training

"He's a madman, he eats human flesh, yet technically is human himself, but barely, he dresses his hair with the blood of his victims and cuts it with a chain saw!" Gladimere informed me.

"So, this isn't all a big joke, is it?" I asked disbelieving him by now.

"No, this isn't a joke, not at all." He answered before carrying on as though it was a normal everyday conversation.

"Darkne normally picks his victims for a reason, before he picked a boy called Lee because Lee's life was boring. Darkne being the sadistic comedian that he is thought he should brighten it up a bit, if you know what I mean. But you? Do you have any idea why he might have picked you?"

He's leaving me a question like that?!

"No" I answered simply

"Your second name isn't like Darkne is it?"

"No, Wren"

"Hmmm, well that isn't like Thomas either, your life's not in anyway... boring?" He questioned.

"No, not particularly"

"Well, there's no obvious sign of why he chose you but he always has some kind of twisted reason" He said, thinking. "With my help you can defeat him" He added.

"Good, how?"

"Magic, I could teach you maybe. If you are very lucky you will be able to control magic" He explained.

"ME?! Control magic? Look mate, I'm really not sure I'm buying any of this, let alone normal people like us being able to use magic!" I chuckled at the idea.

He nodded a bemused look on his creased face.

"I'm not trying to sell you anything Danny" His expression was as if made out of stone, not a single crack revealed any sign of him joking around or playing a game.

"Ok, so I'll have to learn magic" Trying to sound professional.

"It is the only way to prevent your death. Now, we must do this quickly. Here's your first test" he finished then pointed to a cup full of water standing on the table "Drain it" He ordered.

I blinked. "What?!"

He repeated his instruction. I stared at him unconvinced.

"How? I should like drink it?"

"No" He tutted "By using magic, if you have the power it should be easy and may even come naturally to you, if you don't have the power however…"

I stare back grimacing, it wouldn't work for sure! Magic couldn't be real… regardless I picked up the cup and waved over the top of it imagining a TV magician, nothing happened. I looked up at Gladimere, he nodded at the cup. I sighed but tried again telling the liquid, inside my brain, to leave the cup. The words burst out of my mouth. "Leave!!!" I ordered out loud. "Leave!! Now, I order you!!" I bellowed like a king banishing scum from his castle, the cup shot across the table spilling the water over the floor. Gladimere jumped up surprised.

"Wow! I wasn't expecting that, that was so quick... and good technique, different way of doing it anyway!" He praised

"Whoa!" I shouted staring at the pushed over cup. "Did I just do that?"

"Yes, yes you did. You have the power. Now, next test" He obviously wasn't wasting any time, at that second he fell backwards into the chair his body slumping lazily, darkness hit his face, spreading over his features like a plague turning it sinister and evil, his eyes closed. I leant forward towards him and in a flash his eyes flicked open then he stood shouting.

"This!!!"

I coughed then spluttered, grabbing the sides of the table tight, I tried to breath but couldn't, a ball of rock had formed in my throat, I started to choke! No! I was going to die!! A power built up deep inside me then exploded outwards, An intense heat was created in my mouth, I felt the rock melt and become liquid within seconds which slid down my gullet smoothly like fresh water, I sat up gasping for breath, I did it! Gladimere remained possessed for a few seconds then returned to normal, his face lightening again, the malevolence draining away.

"Oh no! Did I hurt you?!" He examined me for a brief moment then continued, realizing I was alright. "I think somehow Darkne had caught me unaware and took my body for his own, his magic must have over whelmed me." He spluttered. "But you survived. You just survived an attack from the great lord Darkne" He laughed joyfully

49

then sat for a few seconds in thoughtful silence before speaking again.

"I think! I think... Thomas Darkne chose you because...he saw you as a challenge!"

Chapter five: I've got the power!

Gladimere taught me how to set objects alight, he said it would be
harder to set alight to Thomas Darkne because he is more powerful
and can fight it off with his own magic by using a cooling spell or
something similar to counter it. He also taught me how to freeze
water and control stuff like rocks and grass with my mind and fling
them at other things like Darkne of course. Gladimere said that I was
catching up pretty well, he didn't have to praise me all the time
though, I wasn't a kid! Although he treated me like a child he did help
me with controlling magic which is the only thing that can keep me
alive. Over the past day my entire mind set had been turned inside
out, magic most definitely existed! And I didn't even have time to
marvel at that fact, it was time to get back and prepare for the fight of
my life.

So, on my way back home, this is when the next round of chaos
happens. On the bus, it was crowded with people, all tired from a
long day of work, stressed out, hot and bothered. I was sitting at the
front watching the driver jump each time we went over a, bump. We
were almost at my stop when the driver lost grip of the wheel!! He
yelled and fell to the floor, hit by an invisible force, before my body
knew what was happening something deep in my mind screamed
"Darkne!" I guessed he must have been in front of the bus floating
above the ground blasting the bus with magic. The driver looked
terrified when he saw me moving towards him.

"Move, I can help" I snapped,

He didn't move so no time to waste I grabbed him and threw him out of the way. I stared at the steering wheel unsure of myself, I hadn't got my drivers license yet... Magic! I placed my hands just two centimetres above the wheel and beams of red light shot out from my palms attaching me to the rubber. I pulled to the left and the whole bus turned! YES! I could see yellow balls of light smashing against the side of the bus. I followed them back to the certain spot where they were starting from and whipped a zap of electricity at it before staring at my hands in disbelieve, the yellow balls of light ceased, I must have hit Darkne! Score one for Danny boy.

"You're harmless Thomas Darkne! You can't kill me!!" I laughed hopefully, caught up in the mad adrenaline, turning the bus down a right lane.

The passengers were stuck to their seats not understanding what was going on hands gripping the supports of their seats, knuckles whitening with the pressure, the driver didn't try to attack me for the wheel, he was frozen to the spot, watching me in amazement. He must have thought I was a god. Something hit the bus from the back and the windows blew out, the vehicle was sent flying into the air heading straight towards a parked car! The passengers were screaming like deranged, singing cats, the driver grabbed onto anything he could, hanging on for dear life, Darkne's laughter echoed through my head.

"I have won that easy! And I thought that you would have put up more of a fight" He said.

"NO!"I thundered creating a huge bubble of energy below us, the bus zoomed straight through the shield but stopped in midair, hanging five feet off the ground. I then lowered it gently to the ground, touch down! The rescued civilians exited the bus one by one smiling with confusion as they passed me not knowing what to say; "Thank you" or "What the hell?" Joining the other bewildered people outside. All saved by me, was it possible for someone to learn magic as fast as me? Surely no one found it as easy as me, as easy as Danny almighty!!

Chapter six: The attack!

Two days later Gladimere sent me an email, saying "Don't go out of the house, eat only food and drink created by magic; which doesn't taste too good unless you're an expert at it, keep away from sharp objects, turn all electric equipment off except the television, Darkne can't help sending messages by TV before he attacks, it will give you time to prepare. P.S. Try to make a strong magical shield around your house that might be able to stop him. Good luck" With that I switched off the computer and turned the TV on.

I started on the shield; I completed it with little trouble but I didn't know if that could hold a magical lord back. I started to run a bath not too hot with a little bit of cold when Thomas Darkne's voice rang through the house although he wasn't shouting.
"Hello Danny boy" Then he sang out the next words in tune to the song Danny boy. "The freaks, the freaks are calling"
I stepped into sight of him on the TV and he smiled.
"Hello, how good to see you again, I bet you've missed me" He said.
"Yes, of course, my favourite freak of the year" I replied.
"Exactly, so, you ran to Gladimere? I'll have you know, he used to be a good friend of mine, are you sure you can trust him?" He asked calmly, I fell silent. "I will give you two hours to prepare yourself for me, I hope you know how to cook roast human, good bye" I switched the TV off. Two hours?! How long did he want to drag it out?!

I went back to the bath and got into the foaming water. Huge mistake!! It wasn't water! I screamed burning all over, just like that my skin was falling off! Darkne had replaced the water with flesh eating acid! Steam was blowing off my skin, eating away at it like a swarm of carnivorous bugs, down to the bone. I was screaming for, bits of muscle dropping off me, the agony was so intense I couldn't even think. Through the pain I managed to mutter a healing spell and tried to recreate my body but the acid was burning too fast, my magic was obviously no match for his. Then in the last seconds of my life I thought of something else, I activated a cooling spell. A waterfall of freezing cold water poured down my badly burnt body and the fires slowly died away. Then only masses of steam remained flowing from me like white clouds caught in a storm.

My body was slowly fusing back together as I crawled across the bathroom floor to check out the damage to my face. Massive holes of torn skin were dotted around, my eyes redder than Darkne's blood shot pair. New skin formed on my face covering the craters with a new layer. I watched my face in the mirror change to Darkne's!
"AHH!" I yelled, falling away arms flailing franticly.
"Sorry, did I say, two HOURS? I meant two minutes. Darn, maybe I should have gone to school when I was younger instead of torturing poor, innocent people. Oh well, now you will die!" He grinned menacingly. "Darkne never breaks a promise".

☐

☐

Chapter seven: RUN!

I heard the kettle boil, making that clicking noise
"What now?!" I roared rushing into the kitchen. "Oh no!" My eyes narrowed, the counters in the kitchen were set alight! Somehow the kettle must have over heated! Or, of course, Darkne did it. I impulsively fired balls of ice at the flames, and they began to die down, but for every one I put out, two more were born. I couldn't win and the flames were birthing fast! The fires engulfed the cupboards hanging from walls and forced them to cave in adding to the ravenous fires below, the microwave exploded, the sink melted in a few mere seconds, me next! I sent two torrents of water crashing into the flames but they were soon stopped in mid-flight by an invisible force field, it occurred to me that Thomas was trying to lead me out of the house! The flames spread past a block of knives and sent them darting towards me as if fired from a catapult, I yelped and fired a ball of magic into them knocking them off course. At that point I noticed I was still naked! Shutting the kitchen door I regenerated a new set of clothes, a pair of jeans and a long sleeved black shirt with a white dragon on it, no time for shoes or socks.

I raced for the main door of my flat exiting onto the landing, then the stairs, I led myself up them and who else but the devil himself, Thomas Darkne, was gilding down them! He spotted me
"Hello again, so now you're trapped? Too bad, you don't have the pleasure of fighting me face to face just yet, instead..." He paused,

sticking his hand down into his blazer pocket. "Fight my pet!" His hand slid back out and he was holding a huge black tarantula, a red skull on its back. It was hissing madly, ready to feast upon me. I yelled rushing past Darkne on the stairs, turning back and knocking him down them with a fire ball, I took him by surprise and he almost flattened his spider, instead it dodged his falling body and flew into the air landing safely on the wall, then it dived after me scuttling behind me, snapping at my heels. I blasted it to one side and reached the front door swinging it open, slamming it behind me on the spider's leg.

I was panting heavily by this time and almost about to collapse with exhaustion, my magic kept me going though, giving me that little more energy. I stomped through the puddles in the next street then flew to the roof tops for safety, losing the spider and his dark master. Gasping for breath I sat down behind an air vent and updated my journal which I had grabbed from the flat before leaving, I don't know why but I had to write down every little detail so people could know about this Thomas Darkne person, it was imperative! No sign of Thomas Darkne or his giant spider, I heard a car's engine backfire breaking the eerie silence so I went to go investigate, shivering from the freezing, icy, cold night air, reaching the edge I peered over. It was a black camper van; Gladimere standing outside looking up at me.

"Hey! Danny!! He called, cupping his mouth like a funnel

"Yes!!"

"Pass me the book will you? I don't think you can finish that now, you will need your full concentration for Thomas, I'll finish it" He explained.

"OK!" I replied after a long thought, at that I lobbed the book down. I caught an evil glint in his eye as he turned.

"You are way too trusting!" He laughed, my eyes narrowed.

"NO!" I cried, feeling my heart sinking but then he smiled, genuinely happy, then burst out laughing.

"The look on your face!"

I finally realized the joke.

"Ok, take care of it" I called turning away from him to face a levitating Darkne and his hungry spider that had snuck up on me while I was talking!

Chapter eight: The duel

Darkne ordered the spider forward, pointing at me, the tarantula snarled and scuttled across the roof, I tried not to panic; I just calmly looked for a way out and spotted my shirt! I noticed its white sketch of the dragon, it seemed impossible but magic was impossible! I drew all my power to my left hand and forced the dragon out from the prison of my clothing, I released it to the roof tops. I swirled it high in the night sky above my head then brought it crashing down as the spider got closer. It smashed into the hissing beast exploding in smoke, the spider soaring through the air in a defensive ball screeching. My dragon reappeared, floating above my head intertwining in and out of its tail, I directed it at the spider, crushing it into the floor, the bug latched onto its tail with all seven legs: one missing from when I shut the door on it. It constricted my dragon and bit down into its cloud-like neck. My dragon went still for a few seconds then regained consciousness and flipped back flinging the spider off of it. The dragon zoomed towards the falling spider and wrapped itself around it, squeezing down tight like a deadly anaconda. The spiders legs thrashed about madly in the air unable to break free from the powerful, crushing grip, seconds later it blew up! Green slime and chunks of hair riddled meat covered my victorious dragon. Now for Thomas Darkne!

"Well done" he praised, clapping his hands sarcastically "But now the games are over, and it is my turn"

With a burst of giddy confidence I sent the dragon hurtling towards him but it went up in a puff of smoke, reappearing on my shirt as a mere useless picture. Darkne laughed.

"I can destroy light magic as easily as you can create it, now. Do you have any other ideas? I'm getting bored and I feel like killing you now."

I soaked in all my power focusing on knocking him over the edge. I fired my energy at his stomach but his hands shot out in front of him and redirected it and instead it exploded at his feet blowing a hole through the roof that was all I need and at that I was off running, within seconds reaching the end of the building.

"Damn!!" But I jumped regardless of the long fall hoping that my magic would pull me through.

Like with the bus I landed in a bubble of magic a few inches off the ground before touching down gently on the floor. I looked up, Darkne gliding down the side of the building after me, I fired two balls of magic at him from each of my hands, his arms flailed out to the left destroying one attack but the other hit him from the right, he cursed then continued towards me not seeming at all hurt. I turned to run again using my magic to propel me faster through the streets just hoping, hoping, that there was a chance of me getting through that night alive: that Thomas Darkne wouldn't catch up with me and kill me. Those were stupid hopes!

Chapter nine: End of the line

I turned corners, past buildings, past on-looking civilians running for what seemed like hours, then my heart leapt into my throat as I reached a dead end! I was on the docks above the river Thames on a wooden pier, nowhere to run! I stared at the water wishing it would disappear so I could carry on running, of course, that didn't happen.

"So, so, so, so sad" Sobbed Darkne from behind me, I span around to face him.

"Peek-a-boo!" He laughed. He wasn't there!

"Where are you?!" I screamed, my voice echoing in the air, my power shimmering in the water around me.

"Right here" He answered "I'm right in front of you…or am I?" He paused.

"Come out and face me," I shuddered.

"Don't tell me what to do…I'm… right… behind…you!!" He shouted into my ear.

"Ahhhhhhh!" I roared, turning around. He reached out and grabbed my throat tight. His eyes were narrowed, starring evilly into mine.

"Now, I'll kill you how you killed my pet spider." He hissed. My hand slid up my side slowly, I lured power to it. I started to choke! Thomas Darkne was laughing. Then he spotted my hand in the corner of his eye filled with a red light.

"NOOO!!!!" He yelled "Don't you DA-" I blasted him backwards, he created a force shield but too late and was thrown into the water with a loud splash, I laughed with relief as air flowed back to me my mind drunk with happiness and success.

I could see Gladimere watching from another pier, examining my battle so that he could write the end of my story and tell it for others to know, for others to disbelieve. I smiled at him but he wouldn't smile back, he knew it wasn't over, not by a long shot! I couldn't stop myself being so happy, I thought I had won, I knew I hadn't but I just couldn't stop believing I could, water splashed again and Thomas shot out of the river like a rocket, floating in the air two meters above ground level drips of muddy, dirty water rolled off him. He bared his teeth and hissed.

"You have humiliated me enough now, and I have let you, but it is over, child's play is over!" He shot four burning bullets at me, one bounced off me, the others buried their selves into my skin I bit my teeth down, fighting back tears instantly going to re-heal myself But Darkne didn't give me a chance, he was really pissed off now! He set the pier alight and the wood burned the flames eating the planks fast, they failed and dropped into the water. I jumped the holes in the floor desperate to stay on land.

I was surrounded, nowhere to go I was forced to retreat until I was standing at the very edge of the pier all the other planks had fallen. The wood that I was standing on burst into flames from either side, edging towards me; I readied myself to jump into the river to escape the scorching flames when I realized thousands of eyes! In the water!! All pupils aimed directly at me, staring. Darkne laughed. "Piranha infested waters all around you, burning hot flames surround you, your killer before you, what you gonna do boy?? What... you... gonna... do??"

Chapter ten: Brave last words

I stared at the flames, crawling towards me from either side my brain spinning, thinking of any way I could escape, I created a force field of water around me and the fires surrounded it blinding me of anything but red orange and yellow hungry tongues. The flames simply went out. Then I saw Darkne on the end of the plank I turned to him.
"So it's just you and me now?" I asked.
"Yes, what unfair odds" he answered. "Too bad for you"
"NO!" I protested defiantly
"Shut up!" He demanded, my muscles froze up, my force field shattered. I couldn't move!

"I've had enough of your talking" He snarled walking forward he grabbed me by the arms, he leant towards me and licked my face from one side to the other then stopped at my right eye, he smiled then before I knew what was happening he bit into it like it was a pickled egg, I went blind in that eye, the blood poured down my face and into my mouth. He sucked the remaining blood and yellow gore up, then spoke, still holding my arms.
 "I seem to remember you saying, you're harmless, Thomas Darkne, you can't kill me" He twisted sharply and abruptly to the sides and my arms snapped off, the bones jutted out off my flesh.
"Now you're armless!" He hissed with dark laughter. I tried to scream my agonized, hellish yells but my mouth was jammed shut like a clamp. He struck my crotch with his knee and roared a magic spell, I

felt the jelly from my other eye slowly melt! I shrieked with pain; not able to stop now that his freezing spell had worn off and my muscles were back to life.

The pain was all too much for any human to handle, I couldn't take it any longer, within a split second my decision was made. There was no other way. Just before my eye fell out, just before I went insane with pain

 "If you want to kill me so badly, how do you feel now?! Me killing myself?! Stealing the pleasure away from you?" My lips were trembling from the pain.

"NO!!" He gasped realizing what I had planned, he stretched his hand out to stop me but it was too late and I threw myself head-first into the river of piranhas, I hurtled through the air, water crashed around me, they latched onto me, ripping out chunks of flesh, wriggling around beneath my skin. I was getting eaten alive. Leaving this world, but it didn't feel all that bad. I was leaving happily with a half eaten smile on my face because through all that, all the torture, the pain and the fear I had tricked Thomas Darkne! He had lost this battle!! I had gotten the better of the almighty lord of torture!!!!!

☐

☐

THE END

Torture three: Father Nature

☐

In this part you will be treated to a peek of Darkne's different way of organizing mass murder. He selects a young boy called Dom Drakne just because he has the misfortune of having a similar name to him. This boy loves animals as you may gather, time for Darkne to change his opinion…

Chapter one: Crows

My names Dom Drakne, I love animals, birds, reptiles, mammals, amphibians, insects, carnivores, omnivores, herbivores, invertebrates, vertebrates. Every single one is what I'm basically saying. All my life I've watched them in there natural habitats, bought as many animal books as possible and read all of them, you could ask me all the questions in the world about animals and everyone I'd answer correct. I would probably die if I didn't have my love for animals.

Today I am walking through the town centre, spotting all the animals, not very interesting creatures of course, just the normal selection, pigeons, cats, dogs, and a ferret on a lead, nothing special. Then something catches my eye! A row of crows all perched above me on a house window pane, all beady eyes fixed on me, or so it seems. As I walk on their evil eyes follow, I try not to take any notice but I feel their eyes burn holes in the back of my brain, I move on losing full sight of the creepy birds and shake the memory loose.

Shops full with buyers throwing money at the cashiers in a rush to get to the next one. It's raining quite a bit, the droplets splash down into the packed street, people with umbrellas and long rain coats shelter under canapés, protecting them from the vicious weather. Others sat in pubs drinking, waiting for the rain to cease its rage. I don't care about the rain, we need it sometimes, to live, for nature like trees and plants that keep us alive; not that it has to rain all the time though, my thick warm coat is all I need to pull me through the rain, I slip the hood over blonde hair, which is now dark with dampness. My heart jumps, I spot a crow, it swoops over my head almost knocking my hood straight back off. I shriek and duck in reply, then notice more of them!! They're everywhere! Lined along the shop windows spying on me, heads turning as I step past, eyes dead on me! I watch them tilting my head slightly upwards their beady pupils following me not looking away for even a second, this is spooky!

I'm not young and stupid, I'm fourteen and I know what's imagination and what's reality, they really are looking at me. Crows aren't meant to do that, it doesn't say anything like that in my books, sure loads of people think they are creatures of gothic natures but that's just the way they are in films and made up stuff, it's all fiction. A dog starts to bark furiously from behind me breaking me out of my thought process, I hear people start to mutter to each other; the people in front peer back over their shoulders in amazement. I frown, what are they looking at? It looks like their looking at me, just like the crows were! Was everyone going crazy?! I turn unconvinced then gasp, the crows are gathered around me, staring me down from all sides, they've surrounded me. Dozens of them, all in lines like soldiers about to set off in a march. The dogs around them straining their leads almost snapping them selves free, their masters yanking them back shouting orders, they know something is wrong, sweat drops down my face. The birds step closer towards me, squawking madly, their cries echoing in my head threatening to shatter it, I spin around seeing more, on the canapés, what the hell is going on?! The first line off the crows take off darting like arrows towards me, I scream and fall to the floor covering my head with my arms, they carry on flying ahead. The dogs finally break loose off their leads and race forward barking chasing the wave of black sea then running riot being chased by their owners. I stand up and watch the massive flock of birds disappear into the cloudy, dark, sky.

Chapter two: Eat your heart out

Next day, I had dreams about crows pecking my eyes out. I haven't told anyone about what happened, if I did I'd have to explain it and, I really can't! Today I'm going out with a friend, Connor; he's blonde like me and only thirteen. We're just going to walk around the shops, nothing particularly great, what we normally do on a more boring day out. He arrives early in the morning at nine and we set out, heading for the town. I have got a lot of money on me because it was my birthday a week ago and I was using my cash from that. Connor didn't share my love for animals, instead, he hated them, thought they were pests. We arrive at a toy shop where Connor buys a BB gun, I don't know how he got past the shop keeper, he definitely doesn't look over sixteen! I left with nothing then we moved on to the next load of shops. We go into some game shops were I bought two computer games. Then we went to KFC: All just a normal day... so far!

I sit at the table nearest the window and stare out into the on looking street while Connor Is getting the food, I see something that brings back that familiar spooky feeling, a bunch of crows standing around on the pavement opposite me staring with their round black eyes. They honestly look evil! Now I know exactly where all those horror films got the idea that crows belonged in them! Last time it seemed like they physically wanted to kill me, more are gathering as I sit watching them with caution. We leave KFC later walking straight past the evil birds. I point to them.

"Do you like crows?" I ask

"NO, they're vermin!" He spits

"Well, I know this sounds crazy, but, I think they're following me" I say

"Yeah? That is crazy, that's just you being stupid" He answers. So I leave it at that and we continue to walk, towards the beach, leaving the town behind, entering the rocky, hilly areas on top of a high cliff which over hangs the sandy beach below.

The wind blows forcefully around us like a mini hurricane, it would blow us over the edge if it wasn't blowing away from it, It would knock us over to our deaths! I look around nervously and see the crows dotted over the hills and jagged rocks, spying on us.

"LOOK!" I hiss to Connor. "The crows!"

"LOOK, stupid, they're just crows!" He frowns

"No, they are following me, before, there wasn't any, now that I'm here they've arrived from no where" I explain my worried thoughts growing inside my consciousness

"It's just a coincidence" He replies

"I know its not" I argue, he fishes around in his pocket pulling out a BB gun aiming it at the birds.

"If you're soooo scared of a few birds….I'll shoot them off!" He shouts.

"No, don't!" I cry, but it's too late and he fires a pellet towards the group! One is hit and rolls over, knocked to the floor. The others squawk angrily and fly after us, I start to run, but Connor stands his ground and shoots another one out of the sky, he doesn't realize that something is very very wrong, another second passes and I watch helplessly as the furious bird's crash into him bringing him to the ground. He yelps and in a second he's lost from sight covered with crows. They swamp over him, tearing him to pieces, he yells for help but he's a goner and I see one bird pull his eyeball free of the socket, feasting on the mucky goo inside! They crack into his skull burrowing through like worms through an apple to get inside his head to begin stripping off bits of his brains, the mush slopping out onto their beaks and black feathers, I watch in hopeless horror, the realization taking its time to kick in… the crows are eating my best friend alive!!

Chapter three: The escape

The crows leave Connor as a skeleton and start after me, I let out a high pitched scream and run to the edge of the cliff before grinding to a sudden halt, rocks tumble down from under my feet. I spin around to face the crows that bolt towards me, pointing their beaks in front like spears. I wrap my arms around me to lessen the blow; seeing its too late and there's no other way out, the flock slice through me stabbing me everywhere like a pack of flying, oversized needles. I roar as the pain of the combined force knocks me off the edge of the cliff!

My arms flail about me like wings luckily gripping onto a rock which juts out from the face, I cut my hands on the jagged edges of the rock but I hang on, knowing its that or death, the crows spill over the top of the cliff and surround me like a swarm of angry wasps, pecking at my body all over, the strong wind knocks my legs into the sharp cliff, it feels like my legs will drop off if it keeps it up. I look up at my hands losing grip of the rock, a group of birds gather and jab at my fingers, chomping down the small strips of flesh, one of my hands falls to my side; one still gripping the hard rock. I suddenly have a thought. Now that my hand was by my side, it was desperate but it might just work. I reach into my pocket and pull out one of my games that I bought. I start to whack the birds with the box and some drop to the water below like flies. I throw the packaging of the game at the flock then I launch the other before climbing back up the cliff face.

After a struggle I reach the top and lift myself to the surface smearing my clothes in mud and dirt but the crows are still following me! They swoop at my legs as I get up to run, I pull my jacket off and spin around facing the birds. I roll up one of the sleeves into a ball and smack a crow on the head, it crashes to the ground with a squawk. I lash out at the others still chasing me on hot pursuit. I trip over backwards bringing the coat down on top of me. The birds rip through the material and almost get to my face, but I lift the jacket up so they can't reach me, soon all of the crows are attacking my coat, I throw it into the air, it landing on the bunch of crazy birds trapping them for a few small seconds.

I race for the streets, my body totally coloured with bruises, my hands snipped up like paper attacked by a pair of scissors, my eyes full of tears. I see people staring at me in bewilderment as I rush around the corner, the crows zooming down thin alleyways, exploding out of the ends to get me. I yell a warning to the people. "Get out! Get out! The crows, they're attacking me!!" Then I lift my hands up at them making sure everyone has a good look.
"Run! They've killed my friend!" The civilians retreat back up the streets, some of the crows take over me and go for them, ripping them off the floor, but most still follow me.
I shout for help as they swamp over me, biting me where ever they can, I punch out with my fists, only for them to be covered with black feathers. Now that they have got onto my arms they push me to the

73

floor. I land on my back and swiftly kick upwards repeatedly, desperate to keep them away, loads are hit out of the sky giving me time to escape, I crawl into an alleyway just in time for them to regroup and attack again. It's a dead end! I shriek.

"Somebody, please help me!" but no ones there, I look around for any escape routes, there are none! My legs have given up, I can't stand! Feeling the worst pain I've ever felt I struggle to a shaky, unsteady kneel then close my eyes slowly. I accept with a tear that this is where I will die!!! My eyes roll right over inside my head and my body loses function then all feeling, the crows take me....

Chapter four: Hospital bed

Soon after the attack I passed out and was taken to hospital, I've been here for four days, sleeping most of the time, my fingers stitched back together, recovering well, I've only just got to a point were I can eat and drink and stay awake. I can't understand why the crows left me alone when I passed out, it didn't make any sense at all. No ones had trouble believing me about the crows attack, I told them what happened, Connor shooting them, them eating the meat off his bones, them chasing me. The other victims who were obviously a lot older, the ones who were attacked in the street and survived told the people that I had came running around the corner followed by a massive flock of crows and that they were attacked, everyone's very aware of what happened.

The police say that the only reason the crows attacked is because Connor was shooting at them. They had nothing of MY story, that they were following me and wanted to kill me in particular, they said, 'Crows are just normal animals who happened to be provoked to kill and go mad. It would never have happened If they weren't attacked by that boy'. The shock of Connor being dead has really ruined me, those crows ripped him to pieces, broke into his skull! They weren't normal crows! How could they have been powerful enough to smash through bone like that?! I don't know how, but it's as if... they were possessed! By some kind of powerful evil. Now I'm terrified by crows, not the best or most common thing to be scared by, I feel like a total baby. But I have a full right to be scared of them…right? Well, my best friend was killed by them in not the most pleasant way possible either. When I get out of here I need to get some evidence that these crows are following me, take some action shots and take a weapon of some sort to defend my self against them. All I can think about is getting these crows dealt with, but first I've got to get out of here and quick, before the birds come back, but how?

One of the nurses walks in with some food, roast potatoes and chicken; not very good for the taste buds but still food and I was thankful I could even eat anything after what had happened. She smiles and walks back out so I start on my dinner when a hear something, tapping, like something sharp hitting something blunt, as I'm listening the tapping grows to a loud banging noise, growing in pace. I look around thinking it must be some kind of damage done to me since the attack, was I losing it? Then I see it... At the window! I feel hot, sickly bile rise to my throat and my heart begins to beat like a manic drum, a crow! Smacking the glass with its beak!

"Someone help!" I cry my voice a tiny squeak. Before anyone can come to my aid the glass smashes and the crow storms in squawking madly above me, the nurse from before rushes into the room and gasps as she watches the bird fly around, circling me, she then sees the smashed window and putting two and two together dives for a broom at one side of the door leaning against a wall. She chases after the bird and smacks it to the ground with one powerful blow; the crow flutters around on the floor and chops the broom to pieces making its way to the nurse's face in a crazy flurry of feathers and wings. I sit up and reach for anything I can find. The nurse can't escape without letting go of the broom which will leave herself defenceless so either way she's doomed, unless… I grab a lamp and rip it free from the plug socket, I aim then quickly lob it at the crow, it smashes into the back of its head and brings it colliding with the wall, the bird slides to the floor leaving a smear of blood down the wall with bits of china in its wings it flaps helplessly before dying, blood draining out of its head, making a dark puddle on the floor.

The nurse flicks her blonde hair back and sighs, trying to get her breath back under control; she stares at the crow then at me then back, trying to take the scene in. After about ten seconds she laughs with relief.

"Why did that thing have to attack on my smoking break?" Then she looks at the bloody mess. "

I'm not cleaning that up" She adds, she pauses, looking towards me taking a deep breath in releasing it slowly

"So? These things really **are** attacking you?"

"Well, you just saw the proof"

"But why? Animals are animals… not hit men!" She thinks for a minute, watching me closely, her brain doing cartwheels inside her skull.

"I'll just have to find out with you, my names Charlotte" With that she walks over to me and shakes my hand, unsure, then she smiles.

"This whole thing is crazy but it seems like you'll need all the help you can get and I'm going to help you" She sighs surveying the room and the devastation once more

"I'm with you!"

Chapter Five: No shot Sherlock

I tell her about the crows following me, that they tried to attack me before and that I think their trying to kill me, me specifically, I even told her that because I know crows can't break into people skulls like they did my best friend so I think that they are taken over by an evil presence of some kind. She said that I was just being childish, but she agreed to something, that something must be driving them crazy and that they're not normal crows, she said maybe they where drinking something bad in the water.

I'm out of hospital now, at my normal house again. My mum has been told everything by Charlotte and she knows that there's something wrong with the crows. Some days later someone knocks on the door. I quickly run to it, opening it to a smiling Charlotte holding a cricket bat. I laugh
"A nurse with a cricket bat?!"
"Well, I'm not going to bandage the crows to death am I?" She replies. "Now go get your camera and a bat of some sort"
"Right" I say going up the stairs to my bedroom. I come back down with my camera and a hard back book
"That's your weapon?" She asks
"Well, I don't have anything better" I shrug.
"Are you ready for this?" She asks looking into my eyes
"Yes"
"Even though we're going back…. There?"

"Yes" I sniff.

She takes my hand and squeezes gently, looking me in the eye and smiling warmly.

So we go off in search for crows, not my normal thing to do on a Sunday, I'm sure she wasn't used to it either. We walk around in the open along the cliff tops where the crows killed Connor, I really didn't want to go back there, but we both thought it would be the best thing to do to find the evil freaks. I just had to ignore the graphic images inside my head. Some crows had already started to gather on the rocks around us, but not enough we wait, nervously watching the birds until there is an unnatural amount of them, then I slowly slide the camera out of my pocket, my sweat sticking my hand to the button like super glue, I take a shot! That's enough to make them attack!

They fly forward screeching death threats, one dives for my camera, but I quickly slip it back away from it and knock the bird to the ground with my book, feathers go everywhere. A group swoops down as I take another picture, great evidence. Charlotte jumps in front of me and blocks their path beating each one with her bat, they fly into each other bashing into themselves in a wave of confusion. Soon we are back to back and are surrounded by the black feathered menace. We hit them down from all sides, me taking as many pictures as possible. Soon we have fought them back and we see a way through the masses of killers, we run through the black clouds and rush to the nearest police station and quickly get inside before the crows catch up with us.

Gasping for breath Charlotte asks if she can show something to the two police men, they don't look too bothered at first but then she repeats the question in a slightly different way. Something they **must** see! The men look at each then smile before letting us through to a dark room with steel tables and chairs. The police men sit down one the other side. They tell us to sit down, so we do.

"So, what would you like to show us then young lady?" One asked eagerly.

"Actually, HE wants to show you something" She replies nodding at me.

"Ok" The man says withdrawing across the table deflated

"What is it then?" Asks the other impatiently, I slide the pictures to them.

"Proof that the crows are following me" I answer. They stare at the photos in disbelieve then they look at us again, eyes narrowed

"Is this a joke?" They question.

"No, 100% real" I answer.

"So, how does this man feel about you following him and taking pictures?"

"But, their crows" Charlotte frowns perplexed

"You pair of sickos!" One of the policemen shouts throwing back the pictures. I look at the photos.

"How can that be?" Charlotte trembles feeling all the air rushing out of her lungs.

"I don't know…. But there wasn't anyone else there!"

"So how?"

The photos aren't of the crows at all, but all of the same tall man dressed in long black robes who's standing directly in the middle of them.

Chapter six: Freaky Friday

We leave, jaws dropped, totally confused, not knowing what to do anymore.

"How, did the …the man get in the way of our photos?" Charlotte asks.

"I don't know" I say flicking through my pictures. "He's… in every one, no crows, just this man!"

"But there wasn't a man, no one else was there!" Charlotte exclaims.

"I know, I don't understand" We stop and look around at the street, a huge throng of people are rushing down the road, many are camera men and news reporters.

"Come on, we've got to get this" a white haired woman shouts. The bunch of people disappears around the corner leaving us even more confused.

"What was that all about?" I ask

"Let's go find out" Calls Charlotte, chasing the crowd.

I follow her to a huge gathering of civilians all crowded around something that has obviously grabbed their attention. We barge our way through eager to see what's going on, many people moan and groan as we squeeze past but finally we reach the front. To my utmost surprise there's a kangaroo crouching down facing way from the people looking at the wall, hiding its features. Four zoo keepers are closing in on it with nets and electric zappers. It's obviously escaped from the local zoo from down the road creating this totally surreal scene, that's all, except there is definitely something wrong. "Why is it hiding its face?" I ask. One of the zoo keepers gets up close, his eyes widen and for that split second terror is wrote right across his face.

 "WHAT THE?!" The animal spins around showing its face… or what's left of it, huge maggots are eating through its nose and mouth. Its tongue lashes out and I see long spikes attached to it like scythes.

"MOVE! Everybody move back, give it space!" The zoo keeper roars before being pounced onto by the beastly creature, it snarls like a hungry maniac stabbing into the poor mans face with three sharp ended maggots hanging from its flesh, blood shoots out everywhere, the man beneath disappearing in his own pinkish gore slapping the maggots away screeching like a banshee. A brave keeper steps up behind the deranged animal and zaps it with its shock gun, the kangaroo turns to him not appearing to care about the shock, just then the skin of its face dislodges and falls to the floor revealing one massive brain eating worm with teeth the size of knives, it lunges forward latching onto the mans head before snapping down slicing it off in one simple movement.

A crowd of terrified people run in fear, screaming, causing havoc amongst themselves. The kangaroo finishes off the rest of the zoo keepers and moves off after the scared mob its head spinning uncontrollably the maggot in its skull wriggling side to side searching for its next victim. Charlotte is trembling but she didn't run, she shakes my arm; I blink at the chaos of dead bodies and smeared blood then slowly peeling my eyes away, turn to her.

"Yes?" I shudder

"What was that?" she cries.

"I don't know, but I think that's what has happened to the crows" I answer shaking all over.

"The... disease is spreading?" She shrieks.

"I think... it must be" With that we run to an alleyway and escape the tragedy for a few moments. I look up spotting a flock of crows flying over the building, a lot more than normal.

"Come on!" I shout, leaving no time for the tragic scene to sink in.

"We have weapons, we need to stop this madness, stop them killing anymore" I order, trying to pull Charlotte up off the floor, she looks at me tears streaming down her face.

"This... Is...Crazy! We...must...Stop this!" I squeeze her hand for reassurance and we turn to walk off in the direction of the crows... towards certain death.

Chapter seven: Man in black

We stop, believing the crows must have disappeared far ahead, out of breath we sit on the pavement and look around for signs of life, some people move in their houses, in windows turning on and off lights but the streets are empty, except… at first I don't believe my eyes but then I realize its all too real. I point to a familiar shape, someone dressed in a long black robe, long spiked black hair with red streaks down the sides, he stands on the curb almost as if floating, staring out into fin air not noticing us. I stand with Charlotte, slowly edging our way forward eyeing the tall, pale faced man, his robe touches the pavement and goes around his waist, he wears a black shirt and blazer on top finished off with a long red tie. He still hasn't looked at us, he hasn't noticed us but I'm so close I stare at his pupil from the side, it's pointing straight forward, his gaze doesn't drift, just stays fixed to the same spot somewhere in the distance.

We step closer and closer near his side, I watch his eye lids close, they remain closed for a few seconds then when they flip open his pupil is staring right at me! I scream in shock and fall back.
"I have that affect on a lot of people" He says, in a solemn, soft, quiet tone.
"You didn't think I could see you did you?" He questions. I gulp.
"Yes" I tremble. He turns to me grinning open mouthed. Sharp, shark like teeth, meat of some sort stuck in between them, drool runs down his chin and drips onto his shirt. He **is** floating! His feet aren't

touching the floor! He hovers, his bare feet almost tapping the floor. He drifts towards me slowly, licking his lips.

"SO? Has your love for animals died now?" He asks.

"Yes... now I hate them." An idea flickers in my head "Can you help us kill them?"

"NO! Why would I do that? I make them attack you, you idiot!"

"WHAT?!" Me and Charlotte shout at the same time.

"Well, at least you never thought. I would probably die if I didn't have my love for animals. That's good isn't it?" He says. I pause...I did think that... a long time ago!

"What? Oh no! You did think that? Poor, weak minded child" He's being VERY sarcastic!

"What do thoughts matter?" I scream.

"Thoughts matter a lot, like now you need to think, how am I going to get out of this alive. Tell me, doe's your love for animals die as easily as you do?" With that Charlotte bursts out in front of me shouting at the man.

"NO!!!!! Leave him alone" The mans head turns emotionlessly to her.

"What's this?" He asks "Oh, Dom, you've brought me a chew toy!" He claps his hands enthusiastically together

"Why thank you. I do love the taste of human flesh, but I didn't bring my cooker with me today... oh well, I'll just use...this!!" He hisses, pointing at Charlotte. She squeals, her skin turning red instantly then steaming, she catches alight before my eyes! I jump away from her quickly, her eye balls burn out of her skull and her hair sizzles. She turns to me, crippled on the floor writhing around in agony like a dying worm her tongue melting out of her face, followed by her teeth. A dinging noise sounds then she stops burning and slowly comes to a stop, laying still. The man steps to the ground. "Dinner!" he announces happily, dropping to Charlottes leg before biting into it ripping a chunk out then with his mouth full he shouts.

"Im for you do di" The most English translation...'Time for you to die'

Chapter eight: AHHHHHHHHH!!!!!!!!!!

I can't even cry, I'm too terrified for that.

"YOU EVIL BASTARD!!!!!!" I shout.

"Shut up" He replies "I'm eating" Going down on one of Charlottes arms. I fall to the ground, dead inside, watching this man finish off my friend. When he does, he throws the bones at me childishly "Come on, get up" He orders. I can't move, sick with sadness.

"Ok then, stay here and we can chat. My names Thomas Darkne, what's yours?"

I don't think I can speak but words still form.

"Dominic Drakne"

"OH, well, that sounds a lot like Tom, which my name can be shortened to. What can your name be shortened down to?" He asks casually. My eyes widen.

"DOM! DOM, Drakne!! Tom Darkne!"

"UMMM, Yes!" He agrees. "They do sound very familiar, maybe your fate saw that you would be evil and told your mother to call you something along the lines of Tom, the name of the most infamous killer and maniac in the world and soon in all time!" He laughs.

"That's impossible" I shout, staring into his eyes, I can't and I turn away.

"This is boring" He says quickly "Kill him boy!" He demanded. I frown, WHAT!? Then a black wolf appears from behind him, a red tongue lolls out of its mouth.

"I call him Fang" Tom says sending the wolf forward, it rushes towards me saliva dripping from its bared teeth, adrenaline hits me like a wave of acid and I jump to my feet rushing away.

"Exactly, exactly! RUN! RUN!! That's all your good for" Darkne calls to me. I do keep running, running for my life, taking alleyways as shortcuts, jumping over wheelie bins, getting away from the wolf.

Every thing inside me wants to jump back, stand my ground and let the wolf rip through me, but a stronger more courageous part fights back the urge and I race forward faster. I get into the main street and see the people running from a maggot headed Kangaroo joined now by two crazed tigers, all escaped from the zoo, controlled somehow by the man Tom Darkne. The people at the back were being cut open from behind by the freakish trio. A bin falls over behind me and crashes into a wall, I spin around, the wolf catching my eye, crushing a metal tin can growling at me. I run, then notice it's gone after the other unfortunate people, I'm safe, for now but I can hardly breath steadily knowing it's gone off to kill other innocent civilians, what was happening to the world? It was all going to hell!

Running back to my house wildly, tears flooding out of my eyes. I knock on my door repeatedly before my mum opens it, looking worried.

"Mum, get in!" I warn rushing past her falling to the floor in floods of tears. She shuts the door and steps beside me.

"What has happened" She asks, shaking.

"I can't explain, Charlottes been killed and eaten by a madman, now, he's following me, mum what do I do?" I shriek

"WELL! I won't let him in" Not knowing what else to say, totally over come by my all too apparent fear

"No mum, he is too powerful for you, you can't stop him" I yell running up the stairs half way.

"STOP!" She demands. "I don't know what you're talking about! What should I do?!"

"Run, mum! Get out of the house!" I bellow.

She trembles.

"I can't, what about you?"

"Save yourself" I cry

"No, don't be stupid, you know I can't" She argues.

"GO!!" But it's too late as the crows spill in from upstairs, flying to the top of the stairs. They stop and screech madly, forming into the one, the only, Tom Darkne!!

☐

☐

☐

☐

☐

☐

☐

☐

☐

☐

Chapter nine: Death awaits

"Oh no!" Darkne cries. "It's the crows again, oh well, don't worry, their not as bad as Thomas Darkne, oh no! The crows are Thomas Darkne!" He finishes in a laugh, a sickening, evil, twisted laugh. "OH" He adds looking at my mum. "You bring another chew toy?" He claps joyfully, making his way to her, gliding down the stairs. "NO!" I scream. "MUM, RUN!" Tom goes past me but I jump into him pushing him over the banister. I land on him but he gets up first and grabs my arm, he thrusts ten times in every way possible at an inhuman speed then throws me against the wall. I think my arms broken, but then I realize, it's not broken at all, it's simply not there! I look up and he's holding it, tossing it up and down playfully. "Do you want another try?" He hisses but before he can get back to business my mum collides with him and knocks him to one knee stabbing at his arm with the biggest knife she could find, she keeps up the pace cutting holes in his arm, my hopes start to rise! She can do it! But then he tuts and the knife goes flying out of her hand straight towards mine, a sharp burning pain cuts through me and I look down to see my fingers have been severed! I gasp in shock and pain, rolling on the floor, agony overcoming me.

Tom gets my mum by the arms and lifts her above him, high in the air, her legs dangling below, kicking him. With his other unwounded hand he wipes it over his second, healing all of the cuts, they've disappeared!

92

"Too Bad" He says sadly, still holding my mum in the air. "The more people you drag into this mess the more deaths there will be, already Charlotte is dead, that's all your fault, now your own mother will die, all...because...of...you" Grief washes over me. He's right! If I had fought my own battles Charlotte wouldn't be dead and my mum wouldn't be on deaths door. Darkne grins. "Oh, and did I mention...Connor?"

Right, that was all I could take! I reached for the knife and readied myself to stab, right through my heart. I strike but my fingerless hand is useless and it cuts right off target adding to the agony. The knife melts before I can try again.

"One has already gotten away from me like that, YOU will not, you will be killed by **my** hand" Tom says. "Now, watch as your mum dies!" he rips her in two pieces and throws them to either side of me. I bury my head in my fingerless hand then hear Darkne say.

"NOW! Your death awaits" Then he yanks my head up, he's behind me, he bends down and whispers into my ear.

"Look at the destruction you have created" Turning my head to each bit of tragedy in turn. I can't look away. A hole opens up in the floor in front of me.

"GO!" He shouts, sliding me across the floor on a red carpet of blood. I fall down the empty, deep crater and into complete darkness!

Chapter Ten: The Change of plan!

The air is icy cold; a red glowing light appears and gives the place a dim brightness.

"Kill me then!" I roar as Darkne steps into the red light smiling demonically.

"Yes, it is your time" He nods drawing a long sword. He reaches my twisted body and hacks into my battered flesh. I smile weakly, soon it will be the end and the pain will stop. I start to pass out of existence when Darkne clicks his fingers and my body feels refilled, I'm not going to die! My arm grows back, as do my fingers!

"WHY?!" I gasp.

"I can't kill you" He whispers. "I must keep you alive, I can't kill again! I thought I could carry on, but, the need is filled, the urge to kill is …gone! I can't believe it! What has happened?" He blinks. "I will bring back all of the people I have killed" He explains. I smile relief beyond relief!

"Thank you" I cry getting up hugging him.

"I'm not that evil" He says. He pushes me away smiling kindly then in a flash his features turn menacing.

"Or, I'm not that….kind!" He hisses pushing me back to the floor redrawing his sword. "A death would be too less of a punishment. Your pain would go, but if I keep you alive. The pain will keep flowing" he chuckles.

I feel my head rip away from my neck. There's no pain! Soon I'm watching my own headless body below. I'm hanging in the air! "NOW!" He shouts. "Watch me gut you alive!" He digs his knife into my body and cuts me to pieces, tearing out my heart, ripping it to shreds, eating bits of my body here and there. Then, when he's done he looks up at my head which is impossibly just floating there above him.

"I am keeping you alive, I have cut out your tongue so you can't talk and now, you will travel with me and watch all of the chaos that I create, for an eternity, all those deaths you will have to suffer, you'll have to watch them all, no escaping, poor, poor, poor, poor, poor boy"

The End

Torture four: Love hurts

In this part you will be taken on a hellish joy ride with the twists and many sharp turns that is love, your tour guide… the lord of torture himself, Thomas Darkne!! But has he had a change of heart?!

Chapter one: Love at first bite

Water splashes across my tired, weary face, cold, icy droplets cascade down my skin massaging the areas around my huge gapping scar. Grabbing my nice, new black robe which I sling over my shoulders I stroll out through the tiny wooden door and into the disgusting warm air of summer. Why do I even ever let it get that hot? I reach out and turn my invisible thermostat down ten degrees then continue, who should I torture today? That is the question, there's Gary, he fort through wars but I could show him true terror, make him realize he hasn't seen anything yet. Or Johnny, he's doing well at school, good grades, could make something of himself, could really succeed in life, well we can't have that can we? I'll soon put an end to that. I switch off all other thoughts and focus completely on finding him. I search through millions of mental files in my mind and soon am zooming into his personal documents. He's at home, doing his homework, pppperfect! I feel my lips curl up revealing my rows of yellow, jagged teeth. I make his school booklet flick through pages as if being blown by a strong wind merely to attract his attention then

I lift my hand and draw out words in the sky, they are shown on the paper in front of the boy.

"Homework is foolish, why work so hard now when you will die so soon?"

An instant reaction, Johnny screams then throws the book away, great! An intelligent, young boy giving up on homework, too scared of what the pages will reveal, you can't get good grades if you don't do your homework. I walk through the streets that run along the side of my beach/cave/house. I look at the ordinary people who cower in fear of me, seeing my huge scar and blood shot eyes and long, snake like tongue, not to mention the blood gelled hair and sharp vampire teeth, oh and pale skin and long razor nails. I watch uninterested above the heads of the sweet, innocent civilians. I am getting a bit peckish and ready for some human meat so I follow a bunch of drunken teenagers down an alley way ready to attack. Its dark and no one else is around, I could kill them all and eat all four of them before anyone would even notice then I would be long gone again, way too easy. I prepare to set them alight when they spin around, one pointing in my direction.

"Look!" He shouts. They whistle in tune. "Hey hey sexy!" They shout as one, I raise an eye brow, I'm obviously not the one being targeted here so I turn around and what I see takes my breath away, all in an instant my heart starts to exist again, my mouth loses all moisture and my chest begins to rise and fall rapidly. There walking among a crowd of peasants is a goddess of ultimate beauty, the most beautiful young woman I have ever seen, my eyes can't help but follow her movements, I don't know what's happened to me, my jaw drops like a cartoon character. She disappears behind the wall, the teenagers continue down the alley turning their backs on me once again, but I have found something else that has sparked my interest. I creep back out of the alleyway and look for the lady among the human filth of normal pedestrians; I spot her long, curled, black hair and rush through the people, towards her. I follow her around a corner and down another street, then she stops by the curb waiting for something. I stand apart from the crowd and watch her like a crow. I examine her long, luscious, silk like, hair ending in red blood-like tips, her black leather clothes; she looks like an angel from hell: breath taking! A smooth-looking face but there's something deep beneath, something that lets me know she can handle herself, my kind of a girl. Not a brittle twig that can be snapped. Wait a minute! My kind of girl? I don't have types of female, only tasty or disgusting. What is going on with me? My brain is wrecked!! I've never looked at a girl like this before. Maybe a long time ago as a child perhaps but it's never been this weird. A car pulls up beside her and a man steps out, she walks up to him and their lips brush softly together just before they get back in the car. I feel a burning sensation in my stomach, is it jealousy or just hunger?

Chapter two: Dinner for one

The car disappears down the road, a sudden burst of adrenaline makes me feel like chasing it and ripping the man's head from his body, but I don't, I have a much better idea. I turn back down the road and head down an alley; it opens out into a courtyard with metal platforms hanging from the walls and steel ladders connecting them to the floor. I wait under one of the balconies in the rain that my confusion of dark emotions had produced, until I hear voices, not coming from down the alley but from above, all the better, an easier catch. Two people talk, one says she's going to the corner shop, then I hear foot steps on the balcony, she reaches the ladder and steps down. I wait in the shadows. Drool pools at the edges of my mouth as she slowly descends. As soon as she touches down onto ground level I strike, grabbing her from behind, one arm around her neck the other strapped around her waist.

"You feel tasty" I whisper into her ear.

"RAPE!!" She screams instinctively, somebody rushes down the alleyway hearing her cry for help. I squeeze down my fingers around her wind pipe using magic to break her voice box, then I lean back against the damp wall wrapping my black cape around both me and her, we were now camouflage within the shadows. The confused man appears, looking around for any trouble. The woman struggles but I quickly freeze her muscles with a quick placement of my finger, she tenses then doesn't move. The wannabe hero walks away thinking he's simply hearing things. I wait, making sure no one is around then finally release her, she darts forward but I swiftly knock her legs out from under her, she hits the floor crying, in a flash I'm on top of her.

"Please don't rape me!" She whimpers.

I smile weakly "I do not wish to use you for that" She frowns. I clap my hand over her mouth and slide down her stomach, my entire body alive with gleeful vibrations, laying on her legs. Her tears drench my hands but I do not care, nothing could make me feel sorry for this creature, she is prey, nothing else, the anaconda does not spare a moment weeping for its victims, nor the great white, nor the black widow or any predator such as I. My lips, trembling with dark desire place down on her chest and breathing her scent slowly in through my nose I crunch down, she stiffens and lays frozen as I bite a hole through her. I lick around the edges of her huge wound and stare emotionlessly at her soft face, **do** I feel sorry for her? My brow creases into a frown as I feel my mood quickly melting away into another one of my disturbing moments of character shattering clarity. Something very weird is happening to me today... I've been put off my food. I look harder into her eyes, she probably had a family of her own, children, a husband, mother, father, aunts, uncles, sisters, brothers, I took that away from her without a second thought, I feel emotions that I've never felt before. I run my hand over her face, wiping away her tears. Do I care that she's dead? That I've killed her? All those people who will miss her dearly, I haven't just taken her life, I've ruined all those other lives. I think... I do care... but why?

I begin to turn away, but before I do, I shed a tear, my first one in twenty years!

Chapter three: Jealousy

I drag the woman's body towards the ladder then I sling her over my shoulder, climbing the steps. I get to the top, looking at the door of her house. I lay the lifeless body gently and carefully down outside on the balcony, letting the rain wash off the blood before lifting myself into the air, landing on the roof above. I walk along it, the metal clinking as I move. I sit on the edge letting my legs dangle off the ledge invisible to the human eyes, shielded by a cloud of magic. I watch over my kingdom from above. People rush around below splashing puddles trying to get home and away from the rain as quickly as possible. My normal mind set for the day is clouded over, I feel off, not my usual crazy, blood thirsty self. I barely even ate my food, a mere appetizer rather then a main course and my stomach growls sorrowfully as a result but for the first time in a very long time I fear human flesh wont satisfy me. What in the hell is going on?! I clutch my head with both hands, my fingers splayed so to cover the two halves of my skull, I force myself to focus on a random innocent down below splattered with rain and out of breath from the rush to or from work, my mouth should be slick with saliva by now but I don't feel that same old, burning passion anymore, it's like someone has flicked a switch inside my mind, my face screws up into a grimace.

A familiar car screeches to a halt, the door opens revealing the archangel herself, the weather immediately fades into a sunny summer's day, the rain ceasing to exist, the pavements drying as if the weather had never even changed. I watch her kiss the black-haired man from before then walk off. She looks menacingly beautiful, born to break hearts, good job I haven't got one. I remember earlier: my tears, maybe I am losing my touch. I turn back to the car which speeds off back down the road, the perfect way to prove myself wrong. Without hesitation I rocket down the side of the building, as I land on the pavement I almost smash an unsuspecting granny into the ground, still invisible to humans. I rush down the road after the car then stretch out my hand towards it, I squeeze my fingers down tightly together and make a fist, jamming the cars engine up forcing it to stall. I jump onto its roof just before the car restarts and continues down the road. A strong wind whips across my face as we race down the road. Why is he rushing? He zooms through a red light then soon after he stops. He gets out of the car near a small house then heads to the front door sneakily looking side to side reminding me of some rat like vermin. He knocks on the door before it opens to a young, blonde lady. They embrace then walk off together down the hallway. I make them forget the shutting of the door business, using my all powerful mind control then I slip in behind them, my invisibility wearing off. They disappear into the living room, holding hands. I poke my head around the corner of the door frame and watch them lay down on the sofa …kissing! …I see… even more reason to have him killed. I spot a small kitchenette across the room and head towards it going further down the hallway passing the living room doorway without being noticed. I get to the kitchen and watch through the hatch. They're still kissing, that filthy creep of a man has a smile so content its like nothing in his life could go wrong, how wrong he is! The cheat! I look around the kitchen and notice there's a chicken in the oven, I don't know why that's important. The lady pulls herself up from the sofa escaping from the mans clam like lips.

"I'm going to go check on the dinner"

"OK babe" replies the man also standing up. I turn my head frantically trying to spot an escape route. The living room only has one way out, the door the lady left through. There's no way of me getting out without him seeing. The lady is walking up the hallway now so I quickly dive through the kitchenette; running out of options, and straight into the front room. I land silently behind the man, his back towards me. I wave my hand at the only way out and the door slams shut, sealed by a magical paste. The man shrieks in surprise and turns to me, looking terrified into the eyes of his killer.

☐

☐

☐

☐

☐

☐

Chapter four: Don't make me love!

"How did you get in here?" He shouts his voice a timid shake.

"You left the door wide open; a burglar could have gotten in and stolen all of your stuff. Instead, I walk through the door to steal your life. Care to hand it over, or do I have to kill you the hard way?" I ask.

He doesn't reply, only stares at me blankly his mouth hanging open.

"I'll take that as the hard way then!" I hiss moving towards him licking my cracked lips

The woman bangs on the door. "Who's in there with you?" she shouts, worried.

"Its no use, you can't get in!" I call back.

"Who's there?"

"I am Thomas Darkne, woman!!"

"Tell me what's going on" She demands

"Tell her" I urge feeling that familiar dark pleasure returning to my twisted soul.

The man whimpers then turns to the door. "Nothing, it's just a friend of mine"

Moving as quick lightening I leap forward, I grab him from behind and slit his throat with my finger nail. He falls to the floor, dead, simple as that, so swift I barely realize I did anything; I kneel down and rip out a ball of flesh.

"One for the road" I purr shoving it in my mouth, drooling. Then I head for the wall exploding a hole in it, jumping out into the garden.

The woman gets into the room and her screams echo through the night.

I wait until morning then I set off in search of the woman who interests me fairly. I place each hand on either temple and locate her position creating a map up in my brain, that's how I can watch people who are half the way around the world and cause chaos. Life is easy for me, I can change the weather to whatever I want, I can kill with ease, I don't have to sleep, I can turn invisible and steal whatever I want. I can control humans as slaves and… the whole world in the palm of my hand. I could destroy it whenever I wanted, but why would I do that? This earth is still fresh and there's still a lot of pain and misery to squeeze out first. My good friend, Dominic is always here to keep me company although he can't talk and I can't see him, he is always there, watching the ever-growing chaos. Entering the woman's street I arrive at the house soon after. I look through the first window I find and there she is! She works away in the kitchen obviously unaware of her false boyfriend's death, happy, a heart warming smile made up of two soft, pink lips. I watch her intently for ages before I make my presence known.

"Hello" I whisper. She jumps with surprise.

"Who the hell are you?!" She demands

"I am Thomas Darkne, and, you don't have to be afraid of me, I'm just admiring your beauty"

"Why are you watching me?" She asks her voice riddled with worry.

"Do NOT worry, please, I am watching to make sure you don't get hurt"

"I can look after myself thanks" She answers frozen to the spot unsure of what to do.

"Just think of me as a guardian angel" I say, she frowns not knowing what to say.

"I do not wish to hurt you, please tell me, what is your name? I would love to know."

"Not that I find this situation or you charming in any way, but... well anyway it's Valerie"

"Thank you" I say slipping off back to the road.

Outside her house a wide stretch of a smile spreads across my face, 'What a lovely creature' I think before my smile fades, my fangs grinding together, I can't take it anymore! I get that same unsettling feeling as before as my arms prickle and my ribs seem to tighten around my lungs and heart. This has got to stop! Is this a normal primitive human emotion? Like a sickness, a disease on my soul. I rush down the street my brain tangled in a bemused array of brand new feelings, my entire body tainted with this human illness, what can I do?! Then in a moment it all comes to me. If this is such a human emotion; an alien experience for me maybe the only way I can handle it is to become more human, yes! That's it! But how would I achieve this? Ah, there it is, I must find a human tutor, they could teach me to be more human! Simple! Without another thought I dart over to the first house I see and knock frantically upon the door, as I wait on the doorstep I become overwhelmed with a swirl of hot, burning mist within my mind, it presses against my skull as though trying to escape through the wall of bone. A thin, frail, shaking, white haired, old lady steps out of her house as I think of how I could release this constricting fog and before I know what's happening I drop to one knee in a desperate display of human despair.

"Teach me to love!" I burst out.

Chapter five: Help from humans

I sit down in the living room of shaky woman's house, she sits opposite, she let me in foolishly and most kindly made me a hot cup of tea, I won't drink it, evil human sewage! She sits, eyeing me, terrified; she tries to hide her fear but can't stop staring at the long open cut that tears a hole down half my face.

"Hello" I say waving at her, breaking her out of the trance.

"Err, err, yes. Hello" she murmurs

"Don't be afraid" I say

"Yes, err, no, yes"

"I am just a weird, twisted man, but I wish to change, I was wondering... could you help me?" I pled; I look her in the eye trying out my most sincere expression of all time.

She looks at me, lip quivering. "Yes...you...poor...m...an" She answers finally.

"Thank you. You don't know how happy I am" She looks at my emotionless face.

"Yes I know, I don't look very happy" I hiss. After that I quickly tell her my feelings for this woman, Valerie and catch her up on everything else until she is up to date.

She helps me as much as she can. She tells me to give Valerie flowers, putrid smelling things, and chocolates, mud-tasting rubbish. Apparently every human loves chocolates. She told me to brush my teeth with a tooth brush, I think I used one of those before, I can't remember. She paused at what I could do about my hideous facial scar then eventually told me to put masking tape over it and to wash the blood out of my hair, she even gave me a hair cut, with scissors, I normally use a chainsaw, she said to use gel instead of blood to style my hair. She told me thousands of things, to wash everyday, in a shower or bath, I haven't taken these clothes off in twenty years! She told me to wash my clothes in a washing machine, and iron them, to wear deodorant, to earn money for good food, to use compliments when I'm around Valerie, to eat with a knife and fork and to wear socks and polished shoes. To clean out my ears and wear my clothes neatly. Not to burp or fart, how disgusting, I wouldn't have dreamt of doing that any way! A disgraceful human habit. She listed everything I needed to know about what I wanted to know. A truly great help, if I ever got back on track again I'd make sure to kill her last... just to show how grateful I am of course.

The next day she gives me back my cleaned clothes which she also ironed and gave me gel, masking tape, chocolates In a red heart shaped box, red roses, toothpaste and a toothbrush, she let me use her bath and she gave me some deodorant and a list of compliments and taught me how to use a knife and fork. She said the only thing I'd need was money, I easily took care of that. When she wasn't looking I magically created ten replicas of her ten pound note and stuffed them into my pocket. I thanked her, she quickly gave me a pair of black socks and shiny shoes. I slipped them on and left. Sitting on the grass in her front garden I straightened my tie, brushed my teeth, sprayed the deodorant and threw the tape away, magic would work much better on cleaning up my cut although the tape was just the right colour. Then I gelled my hair up into my normal style only it was shorter this time, black spikes standing tall like giant needles. The second thing the woman couldn't do for me was get rid of my blood shot eyes, I covered my face with my hand and refilled my features, the veins disappeared. So after my transformation I made my way to Valerie's house leaving all that I was behind. This was the new me, and I was happy about it. Goodbye, Thomas Darkne the deranged killer, hello normal, caring, all emotional, Thomas Darkne!!

Chapter six: Lover boy Darkne

Getting straight to it I walk up the path of Valerie's house and knock on the door. It's raining heavily. She opens the door and I'm hit by a wave of immense sadness, tears surround her eyes. She rubs them dry, her face contorted with anguish and murmurs "Hello...guardian angel"

"Hello Valerie" I reply.

"Oh, I thought you would have forgotten my name by now" She ends it with a sob.

"No" I start then I look down at my list of compliments. "How could I forget a name as lovely as that?" I finish.

"What's that?" She asks pointing at the piece of paper.

"It's a...shopping list, nothing of importance. Would you like to go to a restaurant?" I ask bluntly

"OH" She laughs forgetting her troubles for a second spotting my gifts then her expression moulds back into a mask of sorrow, as she remembers.

 "My boyfriend died two days ago" She moans starting to cry, I warm my hands up magically and bravely wipe away her tears.

"Cheer up" I whisper. Then make the rain stop and the sun shine.

"WOW!" She says taken aback. "Your hands are so warm! And..." Her eyes widen "the weather" She gasps.

"So, how about that...erm, date?" I repeat.

"Oh" She falls silent trapped in the dark loneliness of her thoughts, then out of no where,

"Ok... angel" She laughs again, a smile breaks out but mine turns to a frown, how can we get there? AH HA! Oh yeah, I'm sooo great! A cab appears, no not a cab... a limo, the driver controlled by me. The door swings open automatically.

"WOW! That was quick" She gasps again, "But I can't go out like this, I look like a wreck, looks like I've been crying all day, and I have, I've got no make up, my hairs a mess"

I brush a finger lightly against her lips and smile looking deep into her wide, round green eyes.

"You look amazing, believe me, I've never seen anyone or anything more beautiful then you, I've dressed up to try and match your beauty and failed abysmally, you don't have to try."

She stares back stunned, until I say.

"Ladies first" Allowing her in through the door.

"Thank you" she says sitting in. I follow her. Then I make sure she's watching me, I click my fingers and the door shuts.

"Ooo very posh!" That wasn't good enough, the driver starts the engine and begins the ride, I've got it! I click my fingers and the limo lifts off the ground I make the vehicle invisible to everyone else except me and her... and the driver and fill the car with red and pink mellow lights.

"OH...MY...GOD!" She yells. "HOW...CAN...THIS BE POSSIBLE!?"

I smile warmly taking her hand, squeezing it tight, I stare into her eyes. "When I said I was your guardian angel you didn't think I was just some normal guy did you? Don't worry, you're totally safe" I say handing her the box of chocolates.

"Thank you" She says, I notice fresh tears have started to trickle down her cheeks, I wonder what's wrong but she turns and shines a breathtaking smile at me and I realize she's crying with joy. She goes to pick up the box but I stop her, then I magically lift the lid then raise one of the chocolates up to her mouth.

"You're already taking my breath away" She trembles, her lips shaking, not able to comprehend what's happening but loving it anyway. She reaches towards me. I pull forward and our lips touch then we embrace. Everything falls together so neatly and with such ease, soon she's staring into my eyes with amazed wonder. "Who... Are... You?"

"I am Thomas Darkne, your life-long lover" I reply. My emotions are flying around crazily. I'm Thomas Darkne and I've just had my first kiss. At Thirty years of age!

☐

☐

☐

☐

☐

☐

Chapter seven: Dinner for two

We arrive at the restaurant and I touch the limo down, then slide a red carpet out towards the entrance. The door opens in auto and we jump out, she sees the red carpet and smiles at me giving me another kiss. "You're amazing" She cries.

"I've got magic, you're naturally amazing" On queue another kiss. I could learn to love this human stuff. We walk up the carpet to the ordering point, the man asks what we would like to order.

"You know what we want to order" I whisper. He blinks

"Right, yes of course" Then he goes off and we are shown to our seats. We sit down exchanging huge smiles.

"SO, how did you know what I wanted?" She asks.

"Mind reading" I answer.

"OH" I can tell she doesn't know if I'm being serious or not.

"What's wrong?" I ask.

"Well, I'd rather not have someone reading my mind all the time"

"I won't, only for when it will benefit you" I say curing her tension.

"Well, good" She laughs. "As long as you promise" She adds.

"I promise"

The waitress comes around "Any drinks for you?"

"Your biggest glass of red wine" I say sending her back off. I fast forward time with a flick of the wrist and the dinner and drinks arrive in a flash.

"That…was…QUICK!" Valerie exclaims, I wink at her then feast on my rare steak, remembering my table manners, as much as I need the food my attention is drawn away, I simply cannot concentrate on my meal, she's all that's on my mind. After a thousand stares across the table at each other she finishes her meal and we leave full of joy. I actually enjoyed my steak and even though it wasn't human it tasted great. We decide to walk home in the dark, our arms linked as we move, how could anything ever go wrong? Valerie stops suddenly and pulls out her phone from her pocket. She looks at the screen worried.

"Who is it?" I ask, she looks up at me.

"It's Martha" I catch a glimpse of a woman's face on Valerie's phone, my heart leaps into my throat. It's the girl who was with that man on the night I murdered him, a horrible sickening feeling in the pit of my stomach tells me I should have killed her as well that night but I swear I will never kill again, I will live as human as possible as long as I can be with Valerie. She answers the call, she doesn't know about the affair obviously, Martha Is supposed to be her friend.

"What's wrong?" Valerie asks sounding concerned. "Oh, yes. I heard about that last night. Yeah of course I'm sorry about that but we've just got move on" She pauses. "Who will come back… for you? Who?" She listens for a few minutes.

"Oh, they never told me he was…murdered!" My heart jumps a beat, thinking I'm never going to live my killings down.

"HE broke into the house and…killed him!" Valerie says in horror.

"That's terrible, no; they never told me he was killed. I just thought

116

that…no…" At Martha's next few words Valerie doesn't move or say anything, her eyes just widen.

"OK…ok…Goodbye" she trembles putting her phone away slowly, her whole arm on vibrate.

"Is she alright?" I ask. Valerie doesn't say anything, she just lifts her head level with mine face like a zombie then as I'm about to repeat myself she tells me exactly what's wrong.

"You killed him!"

Chapter Eight: Over in an instant

"That's crazy, what are you talking about?!" I argue. She shakes her head in disagreement.

"NO, no it's not!" She shouts. "Martha told me, on the phone, about her not being able to get into the front room"

"What doe's that matter?" I shrug. Valerie gulps.

"She said, the door was stuck, just jammed shut"

"SO, it just got stuck" I say, it's no good.

"NO!"

"There's loads of other people in the world with magical powers, it wasn't me" I lie.

"Don't lie to me!" She screams. "Martha said the voice wasn't angry or horrible, she described the voice as a soft, sad whisper" She explains. I think of how I can get out of this one then I realize, there's nothing I can do to make her believe me, my body sags

"Yes...I killed him" I sigh.

"How could you?!" She yells bursting into tears. "He was my boyfriend, I loved him"

"NO! He was a terrible excuse for a man" I answer back.

"How dare you!"

"He cheated on you" I say finally

"Oh! Don't try that one" She warns

"He did, with Martha. I promise you"

"You said you didn't kill him when you did, you're a liar!" she shouts

"You can't promise me anything!"

"Ok, believe what you want. But ask your self this... Why did your so wonderful boyfriend go to your FRIENDS house, they weren't friends, you were, they were lovers, it was at night. The fun would have continued if I hadn't have killed him!"

"Shut up!" She cries.

"You know I'm telling the truth. Why else would I have picked him? Why would I have killed him and spared Martha? I saw you and him kissing, I thought you looked like an angel so I followed your lovely boyfriend back to Martha's house where I saw them kissing most lovingly on the sofa! I didn't want you to get hurt, for him to keep building up the lies, for him to ruin your life more and more. Your pain would be a lot worse if I hadn't killed him and you found out he was cheating later on. You know I'm telling the truth!"

She blinks, absorbing the information.

"You shouldn't have killed him" She says sadly.

"Yes I know, but now, because of you I have changed, I've sworn never to kill again because of you" She shakes her head.

"I'm calling the police" She says.

"No, please don't" I beg "Don't you understand?! I love you! I've never felt this way before!"

"You can't just get away with murder! Now go! Run!"

I turn away, tears streaming down my face then rush off into the darkness, I'm now on the run from the police, but I don't want to kill or hide anymore. I'm trapped. My choice, give myself up, be imprisoned, without Valerie for years! Or go back to the old normal killer Thomas Darkne. The question screams inside my head, what do I do?!

Chapter nine: The choice

I just keep running! I know there's no other way out but to use magic, the thing I really don't want to use anymore. Police sirens! They are all I can hear, I run to an alley near by, using no magic to speed me up or to help me hide or to hear the sirens off a much longer distance. I'm out of breath standing in the lonely ghost-like shadows. No one's around. The cars speed past without checking. I sigh with relief and head back out into the open, no one still so I continue to walk down the road slowly, hoping no one will rush around the corner and recognize me. I poke my head around, there's one person walking away from me with an umbrella covering from the natural rain, not made by me. The puddles below my feet splash, not so good when you want to be silent. The person in front turns slightly and stops, eyeing me suspiciously. I pause returning the stare ready to run for it when the civilian turns back and continues up the road walking with no care to his destination.

I stagger up the next street then stop, feeling hungry, and of course very upset. Why didn't Valerie believe that I would stop killing? Doesn't she love me? I feel a stabbing in my heart which I can't explain, I must just be hungry, yeah that's it... There's a takeaway café just two buildings down, with my extra large appetite I need to eat a lot more, one whole human would normally do the trick for a day but now I'm supposed to be fully human, I wish to keep that title, humans are off the menu from now on!

I go in looking around at the people all sitting down on chairs drinking, they all stop and look at me falling silent, I must look weird in this place, everyone else wearing work clothes me wearing a newly washed black suit and tie, not to mention the tears around my eyes. Thankfully they soon go back to their drinks and food, chatting again. I reach the counter and ask for a steak.

"Err, sorry sir we're all out of those" The highly spotted teenager says in a squeaky voice looking at me like I'm an idiot, my rage kicks in, I'm VERY hungry!!!

"Well, I suggest you go out now!! Go kill a cow, chop it up then cook it blue, within the next five minutes!!!!!! NOW!!!" I order, shouting at him wildly, my vision going a dangerous blood red.

"Sorry sir, I'm going to have to ask you to leave. I'll call the police." He warns.

"NO YOU WON'T! I'll kill you first, that's a PROMISE!" I roar.

"OK, stay here while I go and call the police" The police? Who does he think I am?! The woman I love has just thrown me to them, I'm hungry and desperate and now this pimple faced nerd is going to call them on me?! NO! He rushes across to the door but just as he's about to open it…

"NOW YOU DIE!" I bellow swinging the door open viciously smacking him in the face using magic. He hit's the floor with a harsh smashing sound, he doesn't get up, his customers start muttering to each other, one brave simpleton stands up and shouts.

"OI, mate, what have you done?!" He sweeps his messy black gelled hair out of his eyes to look at me.

"Shut up!" I thunder, knocking him to the floor with a flying chair. I spin back to the teenager struggling on the ground, I've had enough! I crush his head with the ceiling above and it bursts open, the top of the skull sliding across the floor with intense speed like the lid from a drinking bottle. The customers rush out screaming except from the messy haired man who throws the chair aside getting up and to my surprise drawing a gun and aiming it directly at my forehead with lightening swiftness! My choice has been made, back to the old dark me.

☐

Chapter Ten: The confrontation!

The man holds his gun steady his forehead creasing with great concentration, he's obviously very drunk

"Don't make me! Alcororic never misses"

I smile. "OHHHH, so you are the famous Roric the vampire"

He frowns still holding the gun to my head.

"What!? How do ya know me?" He asks not used to many people knowing his real name.

"Well, I know all your little friends, Victor, Tanya, Zanka. I'm Thomas Darkne!" I announce, his face drops but otherwise doesn't move an inch.

"NA WAY! Where's the scar? The blood in your hair? The make up?"

I stop him.

"I have lately had a make over, now, why are you standing in my way?!" My impatience getting the better of me

"Well if you are Darkne then just move along, we ain't enemies, us vampires tend to keep out of your way and leave you to it but I can't just simply allow you to kill these people in front of me"

"You obviously don't truly believe it's me if you think I need your permission"

"Hey man, I know what you're capable of but just calm down ok? I can't let you kill these innocent people"

I laugh dismissively

"Yes you can" then simply blast a ball of fire at his stomach, he smashes against the wall and lies still, most probably dead
"That wasn't so hard now was it?"
I leave through the double doors, thinking of my next move. I am moving back into the darkness but I'm not happy about it. I have one last option, I need to see Valerie and plea for her forgiveness, if she can learn to love me again I can go back to humanity, if she fails and denies me her love I will live my life as Darkne the murderer, my fate rests in her hands, it's got to be worth one more shot.

I arrive at her house and walk through the door after opening the lock with magic, she's in the front room standing in the centre, staring out of the open window with a glass of wine in her hand. I stop at the doorway.
"Hello Valerie" Trying to sound as nice as possible. She twists around shocked.
"NO, please don't hurt me!" She begs her expression strikes dread into my soul, my heart stings.
"You don't think I will do you?" I ask holding back tears.
"You're a MURDERER!" she yells.
"Yes, and I will continue to kill unless you forgive me" I say not knowing what else I can do.
"I can't forgive you"
"Please! All I want is your forgiveness. It isn't my fault I'm a murderer. When I was younger, about seven, I had friends who killed animals for fun, ripping them apart like savage demons! They forced

me to watch! They almost killed me with the beatings they gave me. They made me kill my mother! They tricked me to eat human flesh!" Something in what I've said makes her pause and take a long sigh.

"Sorry, but you're still a killer" She says.

"It's because I love you I killed your boyfriend, because he was doing you wrong" I cry, she hugs me. "It's not your fault about the past, but you can stop killing" she sobs, I look into her eyes.

"Only if you can love me again" I whisper, my eyes sparkling with tears as I search for forgiveness in hers.

"But it's your choice!"

"NO! I can't stop doing all the things that make me who I am unless I do it for you" I argue. She breathes, her body shaking with emotion, she sighs again, our eyes locked.

"OK then, I can love you, if you stop killing!" She says giving in at last, my lip trembles. "Thank you" I cry. No more evil Darkne!

Then she pushes me back

"Wait a minute, just now you said…" She stops herself

"What?" I question, looking at her confused.

"You said you ate human flesh" Her wide eyes can barely handle looking at me now.

"Yes but not anymore!" I say in defence.

"You mean you tried it again after they tricked you? What do you mean not anymore?" Fear mixed with disgust fills her face, no room for anything else, I hesitate, I could lie, I could even use my powers to make her forget, to make her not care, to make her love me how I am… but I want her to love me for who she is…

"I developed a taste for it, it was the best thing in my life until you. Please!" I beg, my eyes staring hard at the ground, I can't bring myself to look at her fearful face anymore. "Just love me"

"NO WAY! I can't love a man who eats human flesh! YOU KISSED ME!!!" She wipes her lips, looks like she's about to throw up.

"NO! PLEASE!! LOVE ME!!!" I beg. "DON'T MAKE ME KILL AGAIN! I'LL HAVE TO KILL YOU!" I say breaking down. She pauses, looks into my eyes so I can understand the brutal harshness then she says slowly and with cold, hatred ridden disgust.

"I would rather die then taste your lips ever again!" She's not lying,

"PLEASE!" Then something snaps within me and I give up, accepting things for how they are, I transform my appearance to it's original glory within a few brief moments and stretch out my hand at arms length. She watches in horror as my hand slowly deforms, twisting and mangling into a long, jagged, rusted knife.

"You broke my heart, so now I'll have to break yours, really break it!" I say. "Goodbye"

She spits at me and my last tear rolls down my face and I drive the knife directly through her heart, I hug her to my chest then drop her to the floor, before looking down at her dead features.

"Love hurts" I whisper venomously then drift off into the night dispelling all thoughts of redemption, ready to live the rest of my life a maniac, a murder, a monster, as the infamous Thomas Darkne!...

The End

I would just like to say a special thank you to Aunty Law and Uncle Danny who bought me the book I wrote this entire story in on my thirteen birthday, although you'll probably regret this later on don't worry… I'll never stop writing! Xxx

Also a big thank you to Mr Woods who was the only teacher at my school with enough time on his hands to help proof read this book ☺ Just joking!

Bonus features One:

Hi, it's me, no not Thomas Darkne, Luke Crook, the author of this book, I really do hope you've enjoyed reading it so far, but if you haven't don't worry, there's not too much more to go. I just wanted to spend a little time between stories to make this book a little bit more personal, let you get to know me, if you don't want to then tough! You've bought it now! No refunds! My inspirations for writing something like this first came to me after reading the first book in a long saga 'Lord Loss' By Darren Shan, after this one I then hunted down every other book he had ever written and devoured them too! Another one of my favourite authors is the amazing Charlie Higson! Look em up! The idea for Thomas Darkne was loosely inspired by the extraordinary Hannibal Lector but of course I hope you all agree he isn't a complete rip off!

I wanted to start my series with something small, only a few short stories to begin with but hopefully you'll be pleased to learn as the series goes on the books get longer and longer and better and better. Characters I hope you enjoyed are of course Thomas Darkne himself and Gladimere because they will be back and featured quite heavily throughout the saga along with a few other characters I can't mention because it would simply give away too much! Now for just a few random fun facts about this story and I'll let you carry on!...

Fun Facts

- _The house Lee moves into is based on a house I spent a holiday to Newquay in just opposite the golden sand of one of it's many beaches. This was also the holiday I spent my thirteenth birthday and received the book I wrote this story in._

- _The character of Danny is actually based on my uncle, Uncle Danny who used to work in comet but otherwise didn't get up to many of the same things featured in the story or so I think._

- _The entire third story is set in Newquay which inspired the high street and the cliffs he clings to after his friend is eaten alive._

- _Originally Darkne was going to have a taxi turn up to take Valerie and him on his date but it took me several years of my life to realise a limo would actually probably be a bit more romantic and more Darkne's style. Finally, did you notice that when Martha called Valerie she only mentioned the voice and the door being stuck not the more obvious detail that involved the wall having a massive hole exploded in it? Well maybe you'll find out why eventually… but not now! MWAH HA HA!!_

Well I hope that didn't annoy you too much, now I'm sure you're eagerly awaiting my next poor excuse of a story so go ahead! Turn the page!

Trails of

Death

The deaths are building up and the police are left useless after discovered corpses disappear one by one. The murderer leaves no signs for them, nothing to chase, the bodies pile up and the mystery gets worse. Soon only the VIPERS, vampire hunters, can stop the killings. But do vampires really exist? Or is it much much worse?

One: The sightings!

It was a terrible day, simple as that. An evil presence lingered in the air strangling all hope and joy from any unfortunate person that stumbled blindly upon the death scene, the stench of a mangled; rotting corpse filled the air suffocating it. Somewhere nearby a police car raced down the rain covered road splashing through the craters of deep puddles, its screeching, high pitched sirens echoed around the dead shell of the city. The road joined onto yet another when finally the car ground to a sudden halt, the heavy rain pattering down on the windows. The door swung open and a tall, dark figure stepped out into the flooded gutter, his heavy, black boots thudded across the pavement towards the white faced, shaking, ghost like woman. She muttered the words under her breath, pointing a wrinkled, quivering hand towards the bricked wall of an alley.

 "It's down there officer" The police man followed her directions and focused on the wall, running his finger up a dark liquid smeared across the brickwork. He brought the substance up to his face. Blood!

A puddle of red gore lay at his feet, his eyes caught it too late and he backed off his boot making a sickly squealing sound as he removed it from the pool, wiping it against the floor in disgust he turned slowly. He trailed after a line of blood splatters and halted again at an over turned trash can, rubbish was spilled over the ground. He looked further ahead and adjusted his eyes then gasped in shock. The body of a woman, of course this man had seen a lot of death in his life but **never** like this.

"Jesus!" He cursed. The body sprawled across the back of the alleyway was torn open straight down the middle, the ribcage cracked open each separate rib sticking out like white bloodied spears, small pieces of meat dangled off the edges, the pinkish mashed flesh lay slung out from its ripped open chest. Further up the body she had signs of stab marks to the neck, not from a weapon but smaller, deeper. Like fingernail indents, long sharp finger nails like a wild animals, a rabid wolf almost! Narrowing his eyes the police man noticed the smaller details, burn marks all over the arms, burst skin, bubbled, swollen half cooked red meat, black bruises and worst of all…the woman's eyes. Picked out by a small bit of metal or as suggested before, fingernails! Where the pupils would have been two tiny black specs sat in replacement, like they were painted back in with makeup of some sort. The corpses lifeless face expression was screaming out angrily in eternal pain.

The police man turned away pulling out a mobile phone dialling a number. He spoke quickly,

"I need a team down here quick, a psycho's on the loose, he's killed once and no ones to be seen, except the body of course, I kind of wish that couldn't be seen either, burns, bruises and the chest ripped open! Cuts, everything! It was definitely a madman of some sort" he turned his head back and fell silent; his breath caught in his throat, the alleyway was empty! Not even a speck of blood was left, no signs that any murder had been committed at all!

"Right, ok..." He said, struggling to find the words "we have a problem" With that the man cut off.

On the other side of the city in a large, black van sat three mysterious beings, organising a hunt. All three were dressed in baggy, black clothes, an over sized hood hung over their heads and covered most of their faces, a cowl neck masking their mouths leaving only the top of the nose to be seen. A silver chain hung around each neck, a metal snake like symbol attached. They called themselves the Viper's, vampire hunters. A small, quiet organisation all around the world, bases dotted all over the place. These particular three were the top dogs! They were currently listening to the bemused police man after hacking into the phone system like a trio of spy's. Long claw like fingernails was enough to tell them it was a vampire attack. These people, the Viper's thought the vampires were servants of Satan and above all else believed they should be killed, blood sucking murderers they called them. Nothing would change theirs minds, the vampires were evil, that was that, well that's what it said in those horror films, most of them anyway!

One of the men stood up after listening to the call.

"Vampire scum! It has to be! What else could do something so vile?" The other hooded double looked up obediently, awaiting orders like a pair of well trained dogs.

"What do we do sarge?" Blake asked.

134

"We've never known a vampire to act this way" The other cuts in. "leaving the body for the police to find then taking it away in a flash when their backs turned? Are you sure it's a vampire?" Scar was always a one to question his superior. The sarge frowned.

"Well of course it's a vampire!" He almost exploded. "Ok, maybe a new breed, but still a vampire" The three Vipers stepped out of the van out to find the alleged vampire hungry for its blood.

Some way along the road a scream pierced the night. A tall, cloaked, shadow spread across the wall and disappeared in a flash. A short man crossed the damp road by a zebra crossing; he spotted some small specks of blood along the floor, a spray along the edge of the wall, his face creased.

"What's this?" He asked himself bending down examining the dots of red.

"OH MY!" He cried jumping back, he turned his head side to side nervously as if checking he wasn't being watched then he backed away slowly staring at the blood. He got out his phone and dialled quickly in a sudden burst of worry. He watched a shadow slide across the road then it appeared at the circle of light created by the street light.

"Who's there?" He called, covering his face with his arm shielding his eyes from the almost blinding light, the shadow stayed still, silent, standing there lifeless for seconds. Sweat dripped from the terrified mans brow.

"Who's there!?" He repeated, this time his voice was a squeak of fear. The shadow moved forward slightly then just before the man fled Sergeant Venom showed himself. "Don't worry with the police, they can't help" He says waving at the mobile. The fear stricken man dropped the phone as Venom walked off past him. He walked further up the road through the rain where he met his comrade Scar, who was out of breath, gasping aloud, bent double from the effort

"See anything?" Venom asked immediately

"Yes! But not much, I think I saw a shadow, running along the pavement further down here" He paused. "And I think it was carrying another, someone else.

"Hopefully Blake will follow it. It must be the killer!" Said Venom.

"Yes Sarge" After that they ran off, chains clinking wildly, being swallowed by darkness.

Down the road in the opposite direction was a hunched, twisted figure, a long cape wrapped around its body, showing no signs of humanity, totally covered by black clothes, no gaps for flesh to be seen, only two red slit like eyes and a set of sharp knife like teeth. Snarling viscously, bent over a crippled, dead body! Blood dripping from its chin!!

Two: Pursuit!!

A hooded man towered over the hunched creature from behind, laying his shadow over it. The creature's eyes snapped to the dark sheet of blackness and spun around growling like a wild animal. "VAMPIRE!" Screams Blake as the beast slices him around the face in a flash of movement knocking him to the ground with a thud. Blake struggled to his feet groaning with frustration, the monster was gone! Blake sped down the road kicking through puddles, drenching his boots. The black figure ahead was running madly while Blake fell behind regardless of how hard he pushed his body, he watched the animals cloak blow in the wind, it ran like an athlete, far superior to Blake, the creatures feet didn't seem to be touching the floor it was going so fast.

Blake turned a corner and crashed to the floor slipping on a slick, sheet of rain water, his legs slid out into the road, his twisted body laying in the gutter. He looked up ahead and moaned realising the murderer was too far ahead, he had lost it! Damn! Blake was left in the road cursing his incompetence with only the street lamp as company; its light shimmered down onto the pavement next to him setting a haze to the scene. Two head lights shone ahead through the mist and the heavy bulk of van screeched to a halt beside the fallen Viper almost running his head into the tarmac. The side door swung open with a squeak and revealed Scar who reached down to his comrade.

"Come on" He beckoned hastily "This chase isn't over, not by a long shot!"

The bent shape crawled slowly, cautiously over the never ending sacks of rubbish, the vile stench not seeming to bother the monstrous creature. The wide alleyway containing the tip of rubbish let barely any light in making it the perfect hideout for this unnatural being, rats scuttled away in a flash, terrified of the snarling demon, alley cats hissed defensively at the thing clawing at it with out stretched paws. The shape moved ahead emotionlessly, ignoring everything else. The cloak it was wearing had slipped away slightly and if anyone was watching it they could have guessed It was basically human, two legs ending with scuffed black shoes, a pair of grey blood stained trousers leading up to a pin striped shirt and a dangling red tie which swept the drenched rubbish bags of filth. The face of the creature was still hidden under its flopping hood. If it was human it was very well hidden beneath a twisted, evil, freaky appearance.

The figure leapt to its feet growling some kind of jumbled sentence spinning in midair to face the two blaring headlights. The monsters snake like eyes squinted under the intense rays of light; it lay in wait for the van to get closer then effortlessly took flight above its roof, toying with the Vipers. The driver, sergeant Venom, curses aloud. "Damn it! It's definitely a vampire, did you see how it moved?!" He says, believing it flew away using its dark powers; instead the thing had landed softly onto the top of the vehicle with such stealth they didn't even hear.

"It could be anywhere!" Snarled Scar. The vampire, as they called it, thumped the top of the metal shell as if in reply.

"Christ!!" Yelled Blake shaking from the hit. "It's on top of us!" At that the van sped forward then halted against the barricade of bin bags in front. The van reversed and yet again stopped, the wheels spinning pathetically, uselessly against the barrage of bin bags.

Two dents appeared in the roof as the fists pounded into the metal. "We've got to do something" Ordered Venom. "Lock and load!" At that second scar got up from his black, leather seat and lifted up the cushions revealing a hidden, secret compartment filled with heavy artillery. He picked guns out one each and passed them down the van, in turn each Viper slid out the magazine and replaced them checking they were fresh and new, locking them in place then quickly loading. They filed out the van then spotted the creature on the roof. They gasped as one, staring at each other in amazement; jaws dropping further for every second they stood there, the thing had torn the roof right off like the lid from a tin of sardines.

"AIM!" Demanded the sarge. The monster looked up towards the three aligned Vipers.

"FIRE!!" Roared Venom letting loose a flurry of bullets. The creature hissed gritting its teeth but otherwise stood where it was letting the bullets pin into its chest. It didn't flinch but let out an eerie snort of laughter at it's bemused opponents.

"COME ON! GIVE IT HELL!!" Venom repeated with frustration Scar and Blake stood astonished and don't even try to move a muscle, stuck to the ground like brain dead zombies, they dropped their guns which smashed into the ground becoming automatically useless. The sergeant turned flabbergasted to his failed comrades. "What the hell is going on?! Answer me!! FIRE!!" His face glowing red with anger, the two frozen Vipers stood still not listening. It was as though they were stuck on pause while all else moved on around them.

The freaky figure stood on the only bit of metal left on the roof of the van and showed its smile under his hanging hood. To sergeant Venom's surprise the thing started to speak, its mouth opened fast and looked as though it wasn't moving at all, the speed was too quick to follow.

"They will not listen" It said "You are dealing with a supernatural, you only survive because I let you… you will die soon, you have asked for war, I am your enemy, I'm not a person that you should like to have as an enemy." It spoke in a sorrowful tone, a males voice.

"FIRE!!" Shouts Venom dumbly ignoring his "Prey", his finger tightened around the trigger and he fired three more shots through the super natural's ribcage. The monster laughed again, louder this time. "You will not escape, Vipers"

"How do you know our name?" Asked the sarge. The monster tapped his nose with a long, bony finger. Then he pointed at Venom.

"You will die" At those words Venom fell to the floor clutching his hands around his head, an instant agony so intense it threatened to blow his skull to pieces. He gasped in anguish rolling on the floor screaming. Then he suddenly fell silent, regained focus and looked up, as well as the pain the creature had gone!

Chapter three: Stalker!!!

The sarge couldn't understand what had happened, he threatened to fire Blake and Scar but they promised they didn't understand what was going on either, that they couldn't understand why they couldn't move. They weren't simply ignoring orders, not at all. The three Vipers continued their search for the murderer but after the last encounter didn't have any luck at all. It was like the thing had just disappeared from the entire area, could vampires do that? Sergeant Venom was sure they could, and that he knew everything about the night crawlers, or so he said.

 The three Vipers feeling disappointed and disillusioned, retired to their base hidden from civilian eyes. It was lined with endless walls of glass overlooking the underwater scene, a steel path led to a ladder which descended down a deep tunnel and went further down beneath the surface of the sea bed! This was the most secret part of the base, only a few Vipers were privileged to know what was down there, including Venom. He would never tell anyone what was down there, not because he wasn't allowed to but just simply because it made him feel powerful, knowing something they didn't know.

Scar and Blake had returned to their rooms which split off down the long windowed corridor like a series of tree branches. Venom, however, was in the dark silence of the main console room. He wasn't alone but the people around him didn't dare talk to disturb his deep thought. What was going on in the old sergeants head were the disturbing facts of last night. For all the three long years he had hunted vampires he had always killed them after he sent at least one flurry of bullets through its stomach, they were strong and more resilient then mere humans yes but not invincible, this new breed of vampire didn't die through two rounds of bullets, it was a freak!! This really did send him fearful thoughts, if bullets couldn't kill this new type of vampire, what could? There wasn't a doubt in his mind that this was a vampire though, he was too stubborn to think he could be wrong about something as serious as this. And he definitely didn't want to waste time doubting himself, as Venom was most of all impatient.

 A loud shrill beeping noise blurted from the monitor in front of him disturbing his long thought train.
"Oh, for god sake!!" He yelled slamming his fists down onto the screen, reading the alert with frustration. "A vampire on the run, one murder so far" A brave but stupid Viper stepped out from the worried crowd of workmen.
"Sarge? Shouldn't you send your team out, in case it's that new breed again, you've encountered it before"
The sergeant fell silent again then after a couple of tense heart beats "WHO LEFT YOU INCHARGE?!!" He thundered without warning, his grey hair whipping out around his head, his face exploding with a bright red colour.

"NO! I am the sergeant of this base and until someone else proves me wrong I will be for a very long time!" He took a slow, deep breath then turned away from his fearful workmen, speaking quietly.

"I will send Blake and Scar, I will stay here"

Blake and Scar, partners in grime waded through the piles of bin bags clamping their fingers to their noses, eyes darting from each puddle of blood or sign that a murderer had past. Blake held out a round, metal, shining device just above the foot prints. The beeping of the contraption increased in speed as he waved it across sharply. The line on the screen zigzagged madly absorbing the DNA from the foot print made from the super vampires shoe.

" I have it!" Shouted Blake breaking the silence alarming Scar, making him jump in the air with sudden shock.

"OH… good, that high-tech device should find out in no time what this thing is" Then he shared his troubled thoughts "It can't be a vampire can it?" Scar asked

"Well. Sarge wants to think he knows everything but I have my doubts" Answered Blake. "I don't think vampires can be advancing… I wouldn't want to think that, but I guess we'll find out what this thing is soon enough" He said looking down at the device impatiently, it bleeped a warning.

"WHAT!? That can't be!" He yelled.

The screen had the words 'Unknown…something disturbing calculation' scrolled across it. Scar joined him, looking in shook.

"But that can't happen!" Blake shared a disturbed look with Scar then said.

"Only one thing could do this, someone or something with some forbidden power has blocked the calculation, and it has to be very strong. It also means... the thing that did this is watching us!" Their conversation ended with a quick worried flick of the head, the jittery double held their breath.

Venom had had enough of all those other Viper lessers trying to get in on the action, they all wanted to be involved with this new case, finding and killing this new improved vampire. They weren't taking it seriously enough for his liking; this vampire business was dangerous stuff! Killing vampires was a deadly business even before sighting this improved version, things were getting tense, he couldn't help a swamp of sweat building up beneath his grey, receding fringe. Not even the cool spring air of the fresh out doors was helping. Eyes narrowed he stared across the calm, shimmering water and lost himself in his thoughts, how many vampires had he killed? Ten, maybe twelve, and Scar? About five perhaps, if that last one even really counted, and then Blake, only four, he was new, a rookie sure but one of the best Viper's he had ever seen, four was a lot of vampires to have on your kill count especially when you'd only been in the business for as long as him. How many vampires could there be in the world? And how many Vipers? How many Vipers were really at a good enough standard to be relied upon to actually kill any at all when it came down to it? The Sergeant rubbed his creased forehead, trying to release the ever building tension, if bigger, badder vampires started popping up all over the world, would they be able to cope? Before he could get too lost in his gathering despair he turned round abruptly, now he couldn't be certain but he could have sworn he had heard something, no one would dare disturb his peace, Blake and Scar couldn't be back already could they? No, they would have contacted him way before now... must have been nothing. His aging ears playing tricks on him, damn old age! He allowed his eyes to rest again on the calming, soothing, steady movement of the sea. He turned again, his hand bursting into action reaching instinctively to his side arm, but it was too late, he had been caught of guard! A sharp, jagged stabbing pain pierced his chest and he collapsed, his vision fading, just before his eyes became useless a black clad figure stood towering over him, face hidden in shadows all apart from its white, shining grin.

"Looks like I caught you on your fag break old guy"

On the other side of the city lurked the cloaked murderer! It leapt from shadow to shadow hiding from the blinding, burning, bright sunlight. Taking routes through alleys but never main roads (out in the open). Stepping down a nearby alleyway was a postman taking a shortcut, little did he know that the shortcut would cut his life short. The creature dropped from the overlooking building. It landed behind the man who was listening to an MP3 player unaware of the killer who was just about two metres away from him. The monster closed in and raised his claw above the head of the innocent man, something collided with a dustbin far away in the distance, at that the man turned off his MP3 and span around, his face ceasing with confusion. No ones there! Then a cat scrambled out from behind a bin, the postman sighed and turned to his normal route.

The murderers claw darted out from the shadows and tore into the mans jaw, the bones snapped loose and fell to the floor, the next hand grabbed his leg and pulled it out from under him, the man collapsed to the floor choking, spluttering blood across the gravel. Silence in the alley for a few seconds then the man is lifted off the floor, the monsters long, jagged nails slide through the poor mans skull puncturing his eyeballs, his vision blacks out but he still screams in pain, he felt the monsters fingers wriggle through his ribcage searching among his organs. it found its target! the heart! Both hands clamped around it and prised it out, the thing swung the heart around its head and smashed it to the floor before stamping it to pieces. The man slumped to the ground and the creature steps over the body kicking its foot through the man's head, cracking open the skull and sloshing the brain.

The two Vipers drove down a nearby road, disappointed once again, returning to base. People around them looked up into the sky, crying out with fear or gasping in shock, the Vipers watched, bemused, but didn't stop the van, Blake pulled out his phone and prepared to dial the number to let Venom know they were on their way. A big, bulk dropped to the floor crashing in front of the van, Scar, who was driving spotted it at the last second and roared.

"JESUS!!" He slammed his foot down on the brake but the wheels rolled over the body regardless

"That was a corpse!" Gasped Blake who rubbed his neck groaning. Scar swung the door open and prepared to get out, Blake stopped him. "What do we do?" And that's exactly when the doors window smashed and they are rained on by a shower of bullets!

Chapter four: The getaway!!!!

Scar sat back in his seat and turned the key restarting the engine, he forgot the open door and sped off without having to think twice. Blake looked into the mirror and watched down the street eyes peeled for a gun, no one! Just confused people running and hiding, no one holding a gun at all, the back doors are rattled by the next rain of bullets.

"How can that happen?" Asked Blake with frustration; sticking his neck out the window looking for the person with the gun.

"NO ONES THERE!" The wind mirror shattered the glass hit Blake's face forcing him to wind the window up. Scar turned a corner sharply and the door on his side snapped off tumbling into the road smashing to pieces. Blake pulled out a small pistol and loaded it quickly just in case he spotted the assassin. More bullets bounced off the roof pinning holes through it. Blake checked the roofs of the houses nearby then realised that the person must be in a vehicle as it must be going as fast as them to keep up with their pace. He switched his attention to the nearby cars, peering through the windows trying to spot a gun of some sort, most probably a machine gun. NOTHING!!

A loud explosion shook the van and it collapsed onto one side, skidding, a brain piercing screech rang through the air. The back right hand tyre was blown off by the unforgiving barrage of bullets. Blake looked back.

"OH crap!" The car screeched to one side, leaning over. Scar grabbed the wheel and thrust it to the left; his powerful arms were useless against half the weight of the heavy, black van and It span to the right. The car stopped, Scar letting go of the wheel. He realised he needed to approach the situation with a slow and steady pace, he sighed then turned the key and restarted the van. He was thrown off concentration by a smash. Blake cursed and ducked down as his window got blown out.

"Oh well! Screw this slow and steady approach!!" Yelled Scar slamming his foot down hard on the accelerator. The bulk of metal hurtled forward, going well, people were running in the opposite direction outside on the pavements, screaming for help, arms flailing madly.

The van lost control and span to the left, Scar forced it further to the right but again it did nothing, the van rocked and tipped slightly pushing Scar and Blake to the floor. The vehicle swerved and headed straight towards the buildings, it rolled over the curb and smashed into the glass window of a shop, halting immediately. Scar groaned and lifted his head over the dash board staring at the smashed glass. He shook his head and slowly reached for the door handle before realising the door was no longer there! Blake's hand whipped towards his door knocking it open, jumping out in a flash. He span around facing his injured comrade who was still reaching for the non existent handle of his door, blood pumping from a wound on his forehead.

"I'll go after the gunman, see if I can find him" Blake called before rushing off down the road, leaving the wounded Scar behind. Scar clasped his leg and tried to un-jam it from the seat (in the crash it connected with the front of the wheel and the seat) Trapped!

Blake stormed down the street dodging on coming civilians. He ground to a halt at a familiar shape. The corpse of the man! He bent down to take a closer more detailed look. His forehead creases. The bodies eyes have been dug into, black specks like before, filling them in. Ribcage cracked open again like before, heart missing, brain fluid dripping off the broken shell of skull.
"Not the nicest way to go" He whispered to himself. He looked up and realised he had created a crowd.
"OH great!" He cursed as he is approached by the mob of bewildered humans. Blake stepped forward trying to clear them off.
"LOOK! It was just a freak accident, he fell" He shouted, pointing to the roofs above their heads, they look unconvinced at the huge, gapping hole created in his stomach. Blake tutted and barged past, there was a ping and the sound of gunfire which echoed through the street, the crowd screamed and dispersed in a maddened flurry. Blake realised a small bullet hole in the pavement in front of his foot, about one inch away, his eyes budged and he looked up, his eyes staring into the distance. He saw the shine of metal down the road and was off! His legs moved like crazy, moving fast intent on ripping the gunman to pieces, pissed at being made a fool of so far.

His target at the end of the road burst into action turning left in shock of being spotted.

"FREEZE!!" Yelled Blake desperately trying to keep his fast pace, he reached the corner and skidded to the left knocking a man out of his path.

"Sorry" Blake called back, still speeding up the road. The person in front was getting away slowly but Blake still ran, his breath a hoarse, harsh, choke in his throat but he still wouldn't give up, he wasn't the kind of guy who did. He pounded around the next corner still going full speed. He watched his target knock into a group of bulky men wearing white dirt covered clothes who were gathered around on the path. The man ran past entering the building behind them, which by the towering of bricks and planks of scaffolding Blake realised was still under construction and as soon as he approached the men he saw that they were the builders; obviously taking a break.

He almost made it past the blockade but the men thrust out their arms, halting him, Blake struggled then stepped back.

"I've got to get that man!" One of the builders blocked his path completely.

"How do we know that, maybe your trying to kill him, maybe he's running for his life" He grunted.

"NO! He's a murderer!" Roared Blake; his frustration building trying to spot the murderer up a floor in the half constructed building.

"How do we know that though? You don't look like a police officer to me, where's your ID?" Other building workers join in the challenge.

"Look! I don't have any! If you don't let me past, I'll be forced to use force, I can't let you stop me!" Blake warned, clenching his fists.

"YOU?!" The builder laughed. "Against five of us? I don't see your gun, officer" He joked, turning to see his colleagues approved expressions. Blake moved swiftly like an elite marshal artist whipping his leg around, smashing his hard boot into the face of the Un-expecting man. He crashed to the floor with a groan, instantly he froze, his neck snapped like a twig. The furious, shocked men looked down in amazement then back up to Blake

"I did warn you!" Shouted Blake not quite believing it himself, what had he done? But he couldn't stop now, these guys had got his blood boiling and he had surely lost the gunslinger by now.

"Go on! Try me!! Make my bloody day!!"

With that they charged blindly at him, he slid a gun out of his sleeve and aimed it dead at the terrified builders, smirking triumphantly

"Bad choice!" Blake said then without a moments hesitation he pulled the trigger.

Chapter five: One down!!!!!

"Where am I?" Venom grumbled as soon as his eyes opened. The room was completely pitch black, he struggled but immediately found he was tied to a wooden chair, both arms both legs. He tried to force his eyes to gradually get used to the darkness but there would be nothing to see anyway. Four concrete walls stood surrounding him just a few metres in diameter, not much room at all, but the person keeping him company wasn't standing around him and although Venom could sense someone there he couldn't work out where they could be. That was probably because they were hanging upside down above him.

"Where am I? Who's there?!" Venom repeated feeling his heart beat increase in speed and hammer at his ribs.

"That one I can answer" Came a voice, female, Venom noted instantly like the great detective he was, young, much younger then him of course, a teenager, around nineteen perhaps... it didn't matter! She spoke again.

"My name is Sasha, your name is Venom... nice name by the way" She purred playfully through the darkness, Venom lifted his head as far as he could, following the sound.

"What do you want from me?"

"Well me and my friends just wanted to make sure you realised what an idiot you've been! You're a vampire killer! Watched the whole series of Buffy I bet! That's fiction, what do you know about real vampires?! You stupid little old man" The girl spat, he could feel her

154

saliva spraying his face.

"You're a vampire! That's it isn't it?! You little bitch! Let me out of here! What are you going to do with me?" He shouted, his voice echoing in the tight confides of the space. "Calm down granddad, if you knew anything about me and my family you wouldn't be so terrified but carry on killing us and you'll have reason to be! We aren't the bad guys love, what you're tracking is not a vampire"

"Liar! You'd say anything to cover your tracks!" He protested

"Just leave us alone... you're nothing but a small minded fool" The girl warned, her voice fading into the lonely shadows.

"How dare you! I know all about you! You murderers! You think you can trick me! Just kill me now and get it over with, I don't have time for your games" Only his own echo was there to reply.

He fell silent... his breathing seeming now a lot louder in the emptiness of the tomb then it did a few seconds ago.

"Hello? Are you there?" Sweat pooled down his forehead and he desperately fort against the need to wipe it away as it beaded into his eyes. Silence, he waited sure any second his life would be cut short... nothing. Then right before his eyes a blinding light burst into his pupils, he shrieked in shock catching a glimpse of a pale face decorated in black and purple make up, long curled coal black hair hanging down from above, rows of sharp white fangs grinning cheekily at him.

"LEAVE US ALONE!" She screamed.

One man Yelped and fell at the feet of another who tripped over him, his arms flailing about like windmills. Blake darted forward; the falling mans eyes bulging, the nozzle of the gun collided with his forehead, the force sliced right through the bone, cracking through the other side, jutting out. The brain hung loosely around the end, dripping onto the floor adding to the damp puddle on the concrete below. Blake tugged the gun back out and twisted to find the others. To his left one man leapt upon his back yelling manically, his fists plummeting wildly into the back of the vampire hunters head. Blake ripped himself free, throwing the man off before pouncing onto him drawing a hidden knife from his waist. He prepared to cut, raising the knife in the air, when another builder flew into his hanging arm. The knife flung out of sight, glinting as it travelled through the sky, the two fighters rolled around on the cobbles, shouting at each other repeatedly. Blake kicked out at the man and he was sent tumbling across the floor, Blake got to his feet in an instant loaded his gun. He aimed for his opponent who was crawling towards him, desperate to stop Blake firing, the man grabbed for Blake's gun arm and pulled it down so it was aiming at the floor, the worker climbed up Blake's arm and batted his face with his hand, knocking out a tooth! GUNSHOT! Blake moaned and pushed the man back, the worker stumbled backwards, screaming, covering his eye, his shielding hand painted with blood which seeped its way through the gaps between his fingers.

Blake ran forward dropping his gun in the rush then with no hesitation knocked him to the ground with a rough punch to the face, dead or unconscious? He didn't care, Blake stood up right dusting the blood off his knuckles. He glared at the blood shed around him, eyeless bodies sprawled across the road like sacks of old clothes. Blake spotted his knife on the other side of the road on the pavement, he went to collect it, bending down he slid it back into his belt then stood again.

"STOP!" Cried a voice from behind him. "I'll shoot!" It warned. Blake closed his eyes and sighed. Then slowly raised his hands and turned to face the one last survivor.

The worker he almost stabbed stood with Blake's gun, pointing it directly at him, whimpering. He stepped towards Blake, standing in the middle of the road still pointing his gun.

"Don't think I won't kill you" The worker murmured

"Shoot then!!" Blake urged, the workers fingers tightened around the trigger.

"Ok, you're crazy! You killed my friends, you deserve this" He said trying to convince himself.

"Go ahead!" Repeated Blake squinting back at the gun nozzle. The builder pulled the trigger, the gun shot went off accompanied by a burst of car horn. Blake's eyes flipped shut prepared for his death in such a humiliating fashion, shot by a builder. There was a ping as the bullet hit against a speeding cars bonnet; the man got torn apart by the zooming vehicle. With a quick cry the man's upper half was blown across the road, spraying blood in a long gory path. The car door opened and a terrified old man stumbled out, eyes widened looking at the unharmed Viper.

"I couldn't see! He just appeared!" The old man screeched

"You saved my life... don't worry about it." Blake said before looking at the dead bodies of the workers he tutted then moved on quickly taking a leap over the car roof. He blasted through the doors of the building that will now never be completed the glass from the doors exploded as he slammed them against the walls, maybe if he didn't waste any more time he could catch up to the suspect. He glanced around the room, white transparent sheets of plastic dangled down, hanging over a single length of scaffolding pole which ran all the way around the ceiling. The actual ceiling was made from a dark, stained wood. Papers are dragged across the desolate floor by the strong outraged wind which rattled the whole tower. Only one set of dusty, cement made stairs kept Blake company, all chipped away at the edges, rough stones were laid on each single step. Blake approached the hazardous stairs with caution ...

One floor above, the murderous creature crawled towards the landing which overlooked the stairwell, the thing pushed its head over the edge and watched the unaware Viper. The monster stood slowly and raised its pair of claw like hands behind Blake's unprotected head. Blake stopped and quickly lifted his head spotting the murderer at the last second, he yelled and reached for his gun hostel only to find it wasn't there! He left it with the bottom half of the builders body, he cursed as the mysterious man jumped onto his back, the thing sliced into Blake's face, one long, bony finger slid into his mouth, Blake bit down and the creature reached for his head with a second talon, the razor sharp nails dug into the Viper's head almost piercing his skull, Blake's teeth fell away from the monster's finger and the mangled claw caught around his lips, without warning the thing tears through! The flesh is cut like paper, half Blake's cheek missing as the skin fell to the floor. Blake gasped and lost focus, pain overwhelming him, losing his senses he tumbled down the stairs, cutting his back on the knife like rocks. The creature stood upright and licked his bloodied finger then flung his hood back, smiling with satisfaction at his opponent now at its mercy. The monster could kill him now and there was nothing he could do, reaching down it grabbed his head tight then whispered.

"I am Thomas Darkne, remember the name. It belongs to your death dealer" With that the newly named freak Thomas Darkne walked away, back up the steps... why not kill him?

The dazed Blake sat up. Blurred memories becoming clearer, the man standing above him, the name "Thomas Darkne" ringing in his ears. He shook his head groaning. "He's human!" He said remembering slight features, the black hair, eyes, eyelids, eye lashes, lips, fingers, although deformed they are still human.

"Not a vampire! Just a human. I must tell the others!" Then as he picked himself up he heard a sound from upstairs. He couldn't abandon mission now, just because the murderer wasn't a vampire didn't mean he should leave it to kill freely. He turned away from the front doors and walked up the steps after the unusually difficult maniac.

Up on the top floor, the roof of the building Blake stood, his hood blowing about his head madly in the viscous wind, the scaffolding poles rattling harshly in front of him. On the end of a plank of wood, overhanging the street below waited Thomas Darkne. He grinned as Blake approached him slowly.
"Hello Blakey" He purred "Come to see the view? You couldn't just leave and go back to base could you? " Blake stepped forward anxiously,
"DON'T JUMP!" Blake shouted. Thomas looked down perplexed.
"Oh yeah, good idea" Before Blake could do anything he stepped off the edge and fell.
"NO!!" He got to the ledge of the building, peering over the side down at the street, no one was there! Then he heard a deep, long, cackle coming from behind. He bit down his teeth into a grimace, clamped his eyes shut and let out a long, unsteady sigh before painfully, fearfully turning around a tall, dark man coming into full view, Thomas Darkne!

He snarled then asked in his solemn voice.
"Can you fly?" Blake had no time to reacted, he yelped his feet losing grip of the edge, his boots slipping on the damp roof making it impossible to escape the fall.

"NO!!" Blake yelled simply, realising his fate, he let himself drop, falling with the secret of the 'Human' Murderer, to his death!

Chapter six: Capture!!!!!!

Scar made it out of the car clamp, freeing his leg from the wedge. He stood by the van leaning against it, moaning slightly from his ringing head. He recovered most of his senses then pulled out his mobile quickly dialling a number in a burst of worry. He shoved the device up to his ear and shouted down it like a microphone.

"BLAKE!? ARE YOU THERE?!" He repeated the call then pressed the button and slipped it back into his pocket. He slapped his forehead. "DAMN! Where is he?" With that he turned around facing away from the van and stared impatiently down the road, his eyes straining, searching for his Viper comrade in the distance, he spotted a familiar hooded figure, He rushed towards the outline then as he got a closer look he saw it wasn't Blake at all! A blur of dark brown hair, Blake's hair was black. Specks of blood on the long black vampire hunter like cape. A thought crept into his brain. The murderer!

Scar's legs set off spinning in a blur, rocketing down the road, giving chase. The next street it turned down an alleyway, knocked a bin flying across to the other wall ripping off the lid with the crash, the following Viper slid around the corner, he shouted.

"HALT! I am a Viper! I am armed" Then he smashed past the bin and almost dislocated his shoulder. The alley twisted and turned, the runners snaked their way through until the hooded prey hit a dead end! Scar stepped towards his captive cautiously, no knowing what the creature was capable of.

"Stay where you are" Scar demanded, spreading his arms.

"I can't! I don't understand… help me get him!!" The murderer said.

"What are you on about?" asked Scar frowning

"Get out of my way!!" The thing shouted, rushing towards Scar, the fast Viper dived at the monster dragging it to the floor with a grunt. He turned it over and gasped.

"Human!"

"Of course I bloody am!" Grumbled the hooded man trying to shake Scar off.

"The murderer is getting away!"

"WHAT?! You're not the murderer?" Questioned Scar bemused

"Of course not!" The man exploded, the veins in his neck almost popping out of his skin.

"I'm trying to catch him!"

"Police?"

"NO! You know who I am!" The man said pulling back part of his collar. Scars eyes widened

"OH!" He shouted realising his mistake, staring dumbly at the metal snake around the man's neck. The newly found Viper knocked Scar to the side.

"Damn you! Now you are responsible for a murderer getting away!"

"Sorry, I made a stupid mistake, it's just, my partner Blake hasn't returned from his mission and I'm worried for him" The other Viper sits up and groaned shaking his head

"Blake eh? Listen, I forgive you"

Scar looked up quickly. "Excuse me?!"

"I forgive you" The Viper repeated

"OH...thank you" Said Scar obviously taken aback by the way the Viper dealt with that, normally one would bear a grudge for ever if this happened. Scar gave him a hand up.

"Toxic, is it?" He asked.

"Yeah that's right"

"I should have recognised that" Scar said pointing under Toxic's hood at his green stripe of hair within the brown.

"No offence but they should have sent me out on the job of catching this murderer, not you three, Blake, you and Venom" Said Toxic trying not to sound as though gloating.

"Why's that?" Quizzed Scar slightly annoyed.

"Because I know a hell of a lot more about him then you do"

"What?! HE?"

"Exactly. You didn't even know his gender." Toxic smiled triumphantly.

"Well, we didn't need to know that... what else do you know?"

Toxic stopped dead then grinned mischievously.

"Why would I tell you that?"

Scar groaned. "I thought it might come to this, if you tell me all you know, and I mean ALL, then I'll try to get you into our group"

After a long hesitation Toxic's eyes got brighter.

"Great! Well, here we go........"

Across the city, at the foot of a twenty story scaffolding, stood Thomas Darkne high above Blake's body, it was crippled beyond repair his bones broken, all smashed to pieces, spear like ribs puncturing his heart and lungs, neck crushed, but somehow, through all this Blake was still alive. Darkne's hand quivered over his head outstretched, Blake's eyes slowly rolled in his face to where he's standing, the dying Viper groaned, not believing or understanding how he's still alive. Thomas Darkne started to speak.

"Sorry Blakey boy, I thought you were a bird...oops! Won't be making that mistake again in a rush" He crouched at Blake's body then waved a hand over his eyes, they shut immediately,

"Note to self, Vipers... don't fly" Darkne reached under Blake's chin and broke off the bones, unclipping them with ease, then he ripped the head free and held it in his hand, tossing it up and down like a basket ball. He smiled placing the decapitated head inside his suit then with a satisfied nod of his head He walked off in the direction of the Viper's base.

Scar and Toxic were walking together towards their base, Toxic filling Scar in with information about Thomas Darkne

"He murders people, which is obvious. But he is also known to eat people."

Scar thought back and remembered the first killing, when they listened in on the police officer. A female with her ribcage ripped open, the meat inside was mashed up as if it had been churned by

165

teeth! Then of course the body disappeared, that was the murderer carrying her off to finish her off in peace he guessed.

"That makes sense" Replied Scar.

"But I know more, he only seems to eat women"

The first kill was female!

"Makes sense! Wait a sec! I can tell this to the Sarge then we can track down this monster a hell of a lot easier, get to where he'll kill next and stop it from happening!" Scar shouted his eyes alight with new found hope.

"But remember, I knew this, not you" Reminded Toxic. They then continue up the road near their base, completely unaware of the evil behind them.

☐

Chapter seven: Captives!!!!!!!

"Hello boys'" Called a snake like voice from behind the two Vipers, Scar span around facing Thomas Darkne in an instant he turned and ran to the doors of the base. He smashed his fists against the metal, the doors lead down a small, narrow tunnel to the base. Toxic appeared next to him red faced.

"He will kill us!!" He screamed. Thomas Darkne stood still, behind them muttering quick, rushed words

"What's he doing?" Scar asked

"It's a chant he does before a kill"

Something about that didn't sound right to Scar but before he could think too much about it the doors made a beeping sound and they opened, Scar and Toxic spilled in the doorway, the large metal gates shutting behind them.

Two Viper's raced to their aid and dragged them to their feet

"What is it?" Asked one of them, an obvious edge of fear to his voice

"He's out there!" Cried Scar "We need to get to the screens for outside!"

"WHO is out there?" Questioned another Viper.

"The killer!! QUICK! To the screens!" Ordered Scar desperately

Scar Busted through the steel doors of the main console room.

"He's out there!! The murderer!" He warned.

Sergeant Venom stood immediately.

"RIGHT! We get him then!"

"NO!" Snapped Scar. "We need to activate total lock down, he's too powerful!" There was a long pause, every Viper gawped in disbelief at Scar expecting Venom to go mad but instead he held his anger back, what had happened with that vampire girl? He couldn't quite get his head round it but something he did know was that he wasn't dead, and surely he should be…but apparently this thing outside wasn't a vampire, but something worse, impossible though that seemed something told him to stop and think.

"OK" He answered finally. "You wouldn't say something like this if it wasn't a big deal"

The Vipers gasped then turned back to their desks.

"We have some information" Said Toxic. "About the KILLER"

"Not now" Said Venom waving him away.

The screen in front of him flickered on and Thomas Darkne's face appeared on it, he was pulling a wide, ghoulish grin at the camera, showing his yellow bloodied teeth.

"Over here Ouric, sound on screen one" Venom shouted across the room, a tall, thin, lanky Viper with his hood down looked up then rushed over to him, his cloak wiping out over the passing desks.

"Yes Sarge" He said flicking several switches on the old mans desk. The sound went with the picture caught on the camera outside the front of the base.

"Hello pathetic Vipers" Darkne greeted and although he whispered his voice was amplified by the surround sound of the speakers which sat all around on the walls, the watching Vipers shuddered at the sound of his creepy, eerie voice.

"You're all shivering in your big, black, kinky boots aren't you?" Venom turned to Ouric again. "Microphones on now"

"Yes Sarge" Ouric said flicking another switch ignoring his shaking nerves.

"So, you are the killer we've been searching for?" Asked Venom trying to sound professional and collected.

"Of course! Thomas Darkne is my name"

"Good, now that I see your face I can tell that you are indeed a vampire, is this correct?"

Darkne threw his head back and laughed out loud, shaking the bones of every Viper in the room

"Of course I am, Sergeant Venom, of course I am"

"I knew it!" Shouted Venom

"Shut up Venom" Said Darkne softly, his words silenced the old Viper

"Thank you… I am the lord of the vampires, therefore unbeatable. I will kill you all, one by one…in fact-" He gave a smile of deep malevolence then continued.

"I have already started" He paused

"What does that mean?" Asked the Sarge spinning around looking at each man in turn

"What do you mean?" Repeated Scar leaning over at the screen, his heart suddenly kicking up a few gears, beating heavy in his chest

"OH look, its Scar… well, haven't you noticed Blake's absence?"

"NO!!" Roared Scar in disbelief although he knew deep down that had to be the case

"Well I have, how odd you haven't being his best buddy and all…oh, you mean I haven't killed him?" Darkne licked his fingers. "Of course I've killed him" His hand fished around in his suit. "But I've brought him with me so you can say goodbye." At that he pulled out Blake's severed head and dangled it above the camera

"You bastard!!" Scar cried, tears welling up in his eyes

"I've been called that many times" Said Thomas grabbing Blake by the hair and swinging him back and forth like a pendulum on and old, grand clock.

"Will you be able to sleep tonight?" He taunted with a sick chuckle, at that Scar launched himself at the screen, his elbows smashing it to pieces, he stopped then fell backwards to the floor, crying out curses.

"Cut off the mic and sound" Venom ordered to Ouric, he completed the tasks with ease then kneeled at Scar, squeezing his arm.

"Blake was a good Viper, and a good man, he shouldn't have died, not like that, not at all" Scar looked up, tears in his eyes. Ouric added. "But when you take a job like this it is dangerous and even the best die when they shouldn't. You should take comfort in the fact that that murdering scum will die soon and that Blake died doing what he loved"

Scar nodded, clearing away his slight tears, gathering his senses.

"Of course" He picked himself up, Ouric rising too. "I will kill him!" Snarled Scar.

"Yes" Venom agreed touching Scar's shoulder in comfort "But first we must defend ourselves, prepare ourselves for battle against this magnif-" Venom cast an eye around the surrounding Vipers. "… powerful supernatural." The Vipers gathered in a line slowly, listening to their master.

"We must equip ourselves with the best weapons possible…now!" He turned to the organised line of troops.

"Get your weapons this instant! There will be Vipers on every corridor, guarding. The others will sleep, we will need our rest, but sleep with one eye open, be on guard whatever you do or it will mean death for you!" Venom finished.

The line of Vipers led themselves into the next room to collect guns to defend themselves against the unstoppable evil. Venom looked over at Toxic and hums quietly

"You can provide us with some important information as you've said, with Blake gone I think it is only fitting that you should join the top, to fill the…gap. Just to show the enemy that we don't stay down for long, that we have recovered already"

Scar glared at the sergeant then slowly left the room, reluctantly, he collected his gun then went off falling into a short nightmarish sleep…

Chapter eight: The break in!!!!!!!!

"These Viper's are nothing but fools, their leader the worst of them all, how he got these mixed up notions of us is unknown, all I know is that he is too stubborn to see it any other way" The tall, ginger haired, pale faced man said addressing the two other vampires in the room.

"Maybe it's best if Darkne just kills them all" The woman wearing the smart, immaculate suit with gold braids and tails responded. That got her a sharp look of disagreement in reply.

"We should never wish death on humans just because they are ignorant"

"Yes, my love, I know, I'm sorry, I just think of all the vampires they have killed due to that ignorance" At that the third vampire spoke up, he had been leaning against the wall across the room half hidden in shadow, brooding.

"I tried to stop him killing those innocent people that time not long ago, I didn't stand a chance, he made me feel completely helpless, what hope do we have of stopping him slaughtering all of these Vipers?"

"No one can stand up to Darkne Roric, I do not blame you for what happened, you distracted him enough to make him forget about most of the civilians, that was as much as we could have hoped for, you did well… but I agree, we have no hope of stopping him wreaking his petty revenge on these poor, mindless idiots, we have no choice but to step back and let it happen" The trio of vampires shared grim looks one at a time then the ginger vampire continued. "What we must do is prepare for some dark times, once Darkne; acting as a vampire, massacres this base full of Vipers it'll get all the other bases around the world riled up and foaming at the mouths for our blood, things will get worse for us and they will attack with more force then ever before unrelenting. We must prepare for dark times"

The next day everyone was moving like zombies towards the breakfast room, deprived of a much needed sleep. Many who were on guard got no sleep at all, and those who were allowed to sleep got very little sleep anyway, Thomas Darkne's voice still banging around in their heads. The Vipers walked, hoods down, faces masks unclipped, guns strapped to their waists. Scar sat down on a table along with Ouric and Toxic who were groaning and shaking from a night of no rest, Ouric looked across the table at his blurry eyed comrades

"At least we don't have to go out today" He said trying to brighten the mood. The other two looked back and in turn nod like robotic droids programmed to hate their lives. The food drifted over to the tables, carried by Viper volunteers. They peered down, focusing on the breakfast then without warning Scar's face lurched forward squishing down into it.

Ouric laughed slightly. "That's another way to eat your food quickly" Before doing exactly the same.

Later that day Scar was on his bed, laying down, trying to get some sleep, otherwise listening to the Vipers crowded outside in the corridor. Ouric was there, Toxic and several others all muttering amongst themselves, Scar heard everything.

"Let's go and see if the killer is still outside." The voice was of Toxic, Scar's eyes narrowed, Toxic should know better! Scar jumped from his bed and slung his black robe around onto his back. The door buzzed open and Scar rushed to find the stupid band of Vipers.

In the main console room the group of Vipers barged in, they crowded around one of the desks.

"Ouric, you know how to work this thing" Toxic Said, Ouric flicked two switches.

"Sound and visual on now" Called Ouric, the picture on the screen came into focus…nothing! Just the line of hedges and the path of gravel leading to the front doors

"He's not there!" Gasped Ouric

"What are you doing?" Echoed a voice from behind them, the group of foolish Vipers twisted around to see their sergeant

"We are going to look for the killer, he is not on the screen."
Answered Toxic

"Really?!"

"Come and see for yourself"

The sarge ran over to the screen. "Excellent" He beamed not quite believing his luck

"SEE" Said Toxic grinning wildly

"Ok, send someone out and I'll watch on the cameras, everyone else go to the main doors and prepare to lock down if anything goes wrong" Sergeant Venom ordered. "Ouric, stay here" He added. The others left and gathered at the doors.

"Ok Ouric, I want screens two, three and four" The sarge controlled

"Yes sir"

At the doors Toxic began his mission.

"OK, who volunteers to go out?" He looked over at the huddle of Vipers, after a few long seconds dragged by one raised his hand shakily.

"How brave of you Darick" Toxic praised as the Viper known as Darick approached the huge, metal doors then let out a long deep breath.

"Wish me luck" The doors beeped then slid open, Darick gave a quick salute then walked outside, the doors slammed shut behind him trapping him out in the cold. The sergeant's voice blurted out over the telecom above the double doors.

"Ok, Darick, I'll be watching you" Darick nodded and slowly proceeded to the hedge row

"Good, I can't get a camera in there" Said the Sarge

"Nothing!" Called Darick then lifted himself back upright before making a whole sweep of the area.

"I can't see anything" Said the Sarge. Inside the doors Toxic and his crew started to cheer loudly at those words.

"WAIT!" Roared Venom above the ruckus

"What?!" Shouted Darick spinning around in a full circle, the Vipers inside fell silent.

"I see movement, quick! Get inside!! He's coming on your left!!" Warned Venom.

"I can't see anything!"

"Get inside!"

"Sorry, sir but I can't see anything"

"Get in-" The sarge watched Darkne lift Darick into the air and drag him over to the screen, so they are forced to watch close up

"Watch your man die!" Yelled Darkne Sadistically as he pulled him apart with his bare hands, Darick's eyes popping out of his head in shock. The sarge turned the camera off until all he could hear was Darick's agonised screams. Ouric flicked the sound off

"That didn't just happen!!" Gasped Ouric. Scar burst into the room.

"Stop them!"

"It's too late" Answered Venom

"No…" He sighed; defeated

Soon the console room was almost empty, only Ouric, Toxic and Venom remained.

"What is the rest of your information?" Asked Venom to Toxic

"Well… I have found that the killer only kills two people a day"

"Well that's a load of rubbish!" The sarge yelled "He killed three yesterday! Blake, a woman and a postman!"

"That is true, but let me extend my knowledge… He only sets out to kill two, one for fun, one for food, he ate the female and he ripped the man to pieces… Blake, he killed because he got in the way"

"So… this Darkne person only eats female's right?"

"Correct"

"Then, if Darkne stays here, he can't eat, unless he gets in here… do we have any females working for us?"

"Luckily Tasha isn't in today… she works weekends only"

"Good, well if we can out wait him then we can draw Darkne away otherwise he'll starve and I don't imagine him allowing that."

Toxic shuffled in his seat as Venom crossed the room to the main telecom and started to tell everyone about his plan. Toxic watched Ouric switch flips in position then approached him from behind; Venom was busy on the telecom.

"If he gets in all we have to do is out last him, we have all the food we want, this sicko only eats female flesh, he'll start to get hungry and will be forced to leave!" Venom stopped dead, his voice cutting off as he heard a loud gurgling noise from behind him. He turned in shock to Ouric who was kneeling at Toxic's feet, blood pouring in a waterfall from his mouth, Toxic holding a knife smiling, his other hand hovering over a button.

"When I press this button, it will let Darkne in; he will get in and kill you all!" With that the sarge darted across the room, hands outstretched everything seeming to move in slow motion, too late! Toxic pressed the button!!!!

Chapter nine: The deaths increase!!!!!!!!!

"Why?" Asked Venom hopelessly, stopping half way across the room, Toxic laughed evilly then spoke.

"You were a fool to trust Toxic" The voice wasn't his own

"DARKNE!!" Cried the sergeant stepping back in fear

"Yes, it is me!"

"How is that possible?!"

"I have total control over his body" Darkne gloated. "I needed to get someone you would trust like Toxic and make him sound innocent, that's why I filled you in on some useless information about me... I've been using him as a puppet for several days now... clever yes?"

"Impossible!"

"I am a... Vampire lord, yes that's right, nothing is impossible for me" Thomas corrected him.

"Kill Toxic if you must, but the damage has already been done, my real body is already inside... I can multi-task"

Venom pulled out a hidden throwing knife and flicked it casually at Toxics body.

"You use his body no more!" Venom shouted as the knife pieced Toxic's throat, the dying Viper made no noise, just dropped to the floor lying still beside Ouric.

"DAMN IT ALL!" Venom roared, he reached the desk again and spoke hastily into the telecom

"Everyone, the killer is inside the building, be on full alert, blockade the corridors, lock yourselves in you quarters, anything to slow him down, I'm going to shut down some inner doors to halt the killers progress but if your on the wrong side of the doors when they close, it's your problem"

Somewhere deep within the base the first set of doors closed, one Viper slammed against them
"NO!" He shouted, whacking the metal with his fists franticly trying to get through
"Oh no" Hissed Thomas Darkne who stepped towards the unfortunate man, the man stood and loaded his gun then yelled wildly, shooting Darkne furiously
"It won't work" Said Darkne as he waved a hand over the man…silence!

Another bunch of nearby Vipers listened to Venoms desperate call.
"Something is going wrong with the door controls, they are opening and shutting at random, it must be something to do with the killer, I don't know how to stop him doing it, I'm trying all I can" The four men moved off down a corridor which lead to a two section crossing, they heard a door open.
"That came from the right, go check it out" Ordered one of the men pointing down a corridor, one Viper broke away from the rest and trailed down the corridor, he stepped through the wide open door of one of the kitchens and made his way cautiously through the room. His loud anxious breath uncontrollable, shaking in fear he looked

around at the clean counters and racks of glasses. He almost made a full turn of the room when something caught his eye. He twisted around and screamed when he saw Thomas Darkne sitting on an empty side behind the door. Darkne jumped to his feet, the Vipers muscles froze, he dropped his gun and fell towards the killer. Darkne jammed his fingers down his throat and searched further down his gullet; he touched past his left gland and squeezed down tight on it. The vampire hunter's eyes grew ten times the size then the gland exploded, white saliva flooded his mouth and spilled out over Thomas Darkne's hand. Darkne wriggled out his fingers then flicked the Viper on the nose; he fell to the ground spreading the puddle of fluid.

Outside in the corridor stood the three remaining Vipers, they heard the kitchen door slam.
"Is that you?" Called one of the men "Jake?!"
Darkne appeared seconds later
"No, Jake is dead, so are you" He said gliding towards them smiling devilishly, the Viper furthest away span around and crashed into the locked down door.
"Open this door! Open it now! NOW!!" He yelled desperately. The other Vipers started to fire, the one furthest forward got grabbed by Darkne, he threw the gun to the floor, it smashed to pieces, the murderer clutched his neck and crushed it with ease. He turned, still under fire and proceeded to the second Viper.

"Stop your fire!" Thomas ordered, raising his voice for the first time, he grabbed the weapon and launched it at the fleeing Viper, it cracked against his arm and he squealed in pain.

"Open the door!" He pleaded. The sarge's voice sounded over the telecom

"I'm sorry, I can't, the doors won't budge, its no use! I'm sorry"

Thomas Darkne brushed the Vipers eyes and then poked them out quickly with two swift stabs, the Viper squealed like a butchered pig and clawed at his eyeless sockets, Darkne pressed his longest finger against the Vipers forehead, he added on weight, putting more force into it, then intense pressure was created and Thomas drilled a hole through his skin, then his skull, the bits of broken bone slid off his face and smashed against the floor like egg shells. A finger became a hand and widened the crater, soon the whole set of fingers were inside the man's head. The hand darted out of the skull clutching the brain. He waited until the last Viper was watching then tightened his grip; the slime crawled through the gaps in his fingers then gripped onto the floor. The remaining Viper couldn't look away, his eyes widening fixed on the gore, he burst out with tears, for all the years he had worked with the Viper organisation he'd never seen anything as bad as that. It was all silent; Thomas Darkne approached the weeping man grinning madly. "Why hello there young man" He hunched over him then sank his teeth into his shoulder.

"SCAR, are you there?!" Called Sergeant Venom on the main telecom.

"Scar, are you there? Anyway, our plan has failed, Thomas Darkne's only been here for a couple of minutes, he's killed most of us and is still going to be here a loooong time. Wherever you are, go to the glass corridor, there we will make our stand, there we'll kill this devil once and for all!! I'm guessing he's listening to this so this is our last chance… I'll be waiting for you, we'll fight him together!"

Thomas Darkne smirked demonically as he listened to the brave words of Venom then; wiping blood from his chin he headed for the glass corridor to meet Venom and Scar for the final showdown.

Chapter ten: The last stand!!!!!!!!!!

Venom and Scar lead the other surviving Vipers into the rooms branching off the corridor of glass windows, the Vipers hid away so that Thomas Darkne couldn't harm them unnecessarily. If Scar and Venom could kill Darkne then the rest of the Vipers wouldn't need to be involved at all

"If we get into trouble we can use the last chamber" Said Venom pointing to the ladder which descended down into the secret room. A pair of doors were currently sealing off the vault

"Be quiet" Called Scar to the hiding Vipers. "And get out of sight!" Too bad there were no seal doors to protect the rooms, only automatics. The doors shut as Scar stepped back. He could have almost forgotten himself and burst out laughing at all the Vipers huddling, shivering, reduced to sobbing children by the all powerful Thomas Darkne.

There was a rattling coming from behind the big doors in front of them. They turned then nodded to each other, the slung their guns over their shoulders aiming ahead

"Good luck" They whispered in time, kneeling, resting their guns on their knees. The doors exploded open then Darkne was revealed holding chunks of meat, he flicked them off and they spluttered across the floor, he turned to the glass windows looking out into the vast sea. "Great view isn't it?"

"NOW!" Roared Venom, Scar rushed forward and smashed his gun over Darkne's head. Thomas span around and grabbed Scar in midair, Scar kicked madly into the killer's chest, Darkne smiled, showing no pain. He started to talk.

"You know how evil Blake is?"

Scar stopped, hanging in the air, he couldn't believe what he was hearing "WHAT?!"

"He killed five people in one day, I only wanted to kill two" Darkne continued

"What do you mean?" Scar cried

"Innocent they were in fact! Blake was a whole lot worse then me, If I hadn't of killed him he would have killed everyone, even you" With that Scar pulled his gun level with Darkne's head then blasted without hesitation. Darkne hissed, smashing the Viper to the ground, the killer glared at Scar hatefully, five bullet holes pinned into his face.

"NOW YOU'VE MADE ME ANGRY!!" He thundered, the lights above him flickered out and in an instant he was on Scar driving a hand full of knife like nails to his heart!!

"NO!!" Screamed Scar forcing the hand in a new direction, Darkne's claw stabbed into his own arm, Thomas Darkne pulled his nails back out showing five, deep punctures. He then grasped Scar by the neck digging his talons in cracking his head against the floor in a burst of rage rarely shown in Thomas Darkne. Blood poured from Scar's dark hair; he was groaning quietly making choking noises.

Venom who hadn't been in the action for a while shot at Darkne who jumped up and stepped onto Scar's head reaching for the old man, holes were shot out of Darkne's palms until they looked like cheeses but he didn't care, he grappled the end of Venom's gun and snapped it off, it crumbled to the floor.

"Now, here's the warning!" Shouted Darkne taking hold of the Sergeant's arm, he twisted, Venom's arm broke, but that wasn't it, Darkne tore it completely off then batted him to the ground using it as a club. A moan from Scar pulled his attention away. Venom silently opened the door to the secret chamber and climbed down blood spilling from his severed arm, before making a quick prayer for Scar.

Above Darkne clubbed Scar with the Sergeant's arm, Scar used all of his strength and threw a fist at Darkne, it connected with his jaw and he was sent flying head over heels to the floor sliding on a red sheet of blood. Scar saw his chance and fled for the open doors of the glass corridor. He slipped on a puddle of gore and landed on his back half way through the exit. Darkne sat up and aimed a hand at the doors, they immediately crashed shut slicing through the vampire hunter's ribcage, he didn't even have a chance to realise what was happening. Darkne's next move was a glance around the rooms opposite him, he spotted the many Vipers hiding beneath their beds. "NO ONE survives" He whispered, back to his normal self again. He stepped up to the glass and cut a line out with his finger nail, then watched the water seep in.

185

Sergeant Venom set up his best pistol then ducked under the wooden desk awaiting Thomas, he held down on the bleeding stump of his arm trying to stop the flow of blood as best he could but it was no use, he could feel his life draining out of him. The vault opened from above and Venom listened to the dark creature climb down the ladder. When Darkne reached the bottom Venom leapt from his hiding place and got ready to pull the trigger.

"STOP! You no you can't kill me like this" Thomas Said. "I do not wish to kill you either; we could be friends, except theirs a small problem… I seem to have flooded upstairs, clumsy me, so you will die, but I won't kill you." Venom placed his gun on the desk. "Kill me, you've already gotten half way through, finish the job!"

"Sorry, I can't kill you, only you know about me and how evil the vampires are, only you can warn the other Vipers of my madness."

"NO! KILL ME!!" Venom challenged. "You said you flooded upstairs, that means I will die"

"OH really?" Asked Darkne, a glint in his eye

"Fight me like a man" Shouted Venom, almost ordering now.

"Shut up, I'm not a man…I will leave now" Said Thomas Darkne spinning on his heels, he climbed up the ladder. Venom spoke again. "But you'll die! It's flooded!" Darkne carried on up the ladder as if he hadn't heard then opened the hatch letting the water spill into the room below.

Sergeant Venom shook his head with confusion. Then he sighed picking up his gun pressing it to his head, closing his eyes, he prepared to pull the trigger... then, all of a sudden it all made sense! Why Darkne chose to attack there, why he kept Venom alive and killed the others, why he didn't just simply kill everyone on their first encounter. Now he understood the answers were brought to the sarge as if by magic, a magical flash of knowledge and complete understanding, it was all so clear now, he now understood his mission in life. He dropped the gun and slowly pulled out his phone then with a long, deep, trembling breath dialled the numbers, the creepy, unforgiving numbers of " 6 6" the phone rang..........

THE END?!......

A special thanks now to Beccy! Thank you for lending me a laptop with MICROSOFT WORD on it! The exact document type I needed to upload my work to the site I published my book with! Without you (Or the laptop) this never would have been possible. I also remember now I got the laptop so I could type out a decent CV and find a job…oh well! Sorry! xxx

Bonus Features Two:

Hello, once again I hope you are enjoying your read! Should be getting slightly more exciting now, hope you enjoyed the crappy out of their league Vipers cos they'll be back very shortly! Well… Venom will be back, everyone else is dead! I put a lot more underlined comedy into this one, of course it could be read totally seriously but none of my stories are ever completely serious, maybe not laugh out loud funny but there you go! When I first wrote the story as a younger boy I set out to make the Viper's seem cool and like secret agents but after reading it through years later I realized how corny and clueless they seemed and decided to really take the pee out of them!

Fun Facts

- *I didn't really leave any clue of this and decided (for some reason) to completely leave it out but this story was based in American, most of the characters being American except for the vampires and of course Darkne. Venom is from Brooklyn… just thought you should know… don't really make a difference though.*

- *All the scenes with actual vampires In I decided to put in right at the last minute, they began to become some of my favorite characters when I later on introduced them to my books so I felt like giving them an extra bit of screen time before they hit the scene properly for the first time, I even extended Roric's scene with Darkne in 'Love hurts' by a couple of lines.*

Now back to the next and final story! Good luck!...

QUESTION

MARKS???

This is the sequel to the first Viper book, Trails of death, full of twists and Vampiric bad guys. When a vampire gang lord is killed by the skilful Viper Red it only brings bad times to the new base of Vipers. A famous vampire family known as the Vamp's know where the Vipers hide and seek revenge. Darkne shows up in the city after a short break away and seeks out his old friend Venom, but Darkne being the master of disguise could be any character in the army of red herrings. Do vampires exist or is it much worse? The answer... BOTH!!

Chapter one: Disaster

In a split second he darted across the room grabbing for his neck, he wasn't supposed to know!! The other stepped in front blocking his path to the master.

"Die!" The man roared. "I know what you are!" He sliced at the protectors face with a knife.

"Take him down!" Ordered the master. The knife went flying into the second attacker's eye; the one behind the first, he screamed before falling to the floor. The body guards leapt upon him, leaving the other attacker alone to fight the last guard blocking his path.

"How did you know?" The attacker asked the master over the guards shoulder.

"Nothing matters, you die now!" The master hissed. The body guard jumped forward punching the attacker in the stomach, they both crashed to the floor hitting at each other. The second attacker with the knife still lodged in his eye lost grip of one of the body guards and a knee came down upon the blade. It slipped further down and pierced his brain. The man went still, his body now feeling weightless under the three body guards. They stood up, victorious. The first attacker still wrestling with the fourth bodyguard kicked him away before getting to his feet. The guard lunged forward snarling madly, cursing all the words I the world. A gunshot! The guard collided with the attacker, the attacker dropped him to the floor, blood shooting out of the dead or dying guard. The gun wielding attacker turned looking at the other three running up the narrow corridor. The attacker looked back at the master then at the window behind the target

"Damn!" He cursed before running towards the target pointing his gun forward he fired four shots at his chest then raced past him before getting out a device and quickly talking into it.

"Get the van ready!" Seconds later he smashed through the window, splinters of glass exploding outwards.

The three body guards stood over their master's body

"Master?" One said

"I am still with you" Replied the master groaning in pain. Another guard got out a small cloth from his pocket and added pressure on the one of his many wounds.

"NO!" Ordered the master, the body guard stared back unsure, still pressing on the cloth down on the bullet hole

"Stop! God will save me" Said the master

"But sir, god can't hel-"

The master clutched the man's neck tight cutting him off

"Don't you ever say that" At that, the masters grip loosened and he died

"Master?"

The attacker landed outside the window down in the rotting rubbish tip. He walked out into the road stopping a big black van, it screeched to a halt. The side door slid open and the attacker got in

"Good job sergeant Red" Said a man dressed in black robes with a huge hood over hanging his face. "Did you kill the target?" He asked

"Yes of course I did" Said sergeant Red. "I am a sergeant now after all"

"That was only because you got lucky"

Red shook his head in disagreement

"How could you call that lucky? I saved the previous sergeant from drowning in a sinking base"

"Well, however you managed it, it wasn't through skill it was through luck" Argued the other Viper

"Ok, what ever you say"

Red sat down on one of the leather sofa's in the back of the van and slid his hand gun underneath one of the cushions. The driver in front compartment started up the car and went up the road.

The old sergeant sat in the darkness of an empty room, accompanied by only a dimly lit candle placed in front of his wooden chair on the floor.

"I know you're out there…somewhere, I know you're near. Why don't you do as I say and come to me? You know I can't capture you, just… pay me a visit some time. Just turn up from out of no where then I wont be able to plan anything against you." The candle automatically went out. "I know you will be back, I have something of yours … I have some of your power"

"Good to have you back sergeant" Said another hooded man to Red. Red walked through the metal double doors watching all the other hooded workers tapping on their computers, their fingers moving like lightening over the keys, the workers like robots all lined up in seats staring emotionlessly at their computer screens.

"So, have you got anymore info on this gang lord?" Asked Red

"Well you confirmed that he was intelligent enough to know you were there to assassinate him"

"I don't understand that, we made it almost impossible for him to know" Said Red

"No, actually it wasn't as impossible as we had hoped" said another hooded man stepping into the scene.

"Oh? How's that?"

"Well, according to computer research, the Vampire gang lord had another very close intelligence group working for him, they go by the name of the VAMPS. They had been protecting the vampire lord for many years now and must have been watching us some how, they alerted him and now should be after us for revenge" He explained

"Well, thank you for that Rodlack. We have a group of highly trained killers after our blood, that information will help a lot"

"The VAMPS?" Red sighed, thinking. A door across the other side of the room swung open. A long, grey haired man stepped out, his eyes glaring down at the floor as he walked.

"Red, I know more about these Vamp's then most other Viper's here will" He said.

"You do Venom?"

"Yes, I happen to know the leader goes by the name of Victor, Victor Van Vamp"

Chapter two: We know where you live

A hooded man walked over to Red smirking

"I think we've got an extra special mission for you that you'll just love"

"I know he can do it" Interrupted Venom. "I trust him with my life"

"Venox likes to say that was just luck" Red chuckled. Venom shook his head.

"Then he is a fool. You saved my life simply because you are one of the best Viper's I have ever known."

Sergeant Red nodded turning to the hooded man by the door.

"So what is this mission?"

"Well, you and Venom will be travelling back to the masters domain"

"But the master is dead. Why go back?"

"Yes, that is correct. But we want you to check the area for his secret intelligence group. They should be there planning the masters funeral. You should be able to slip in and kill them, maybe even bury them with their beloved master, in the same grave without them even realising what was happening"

"We have to hit them now before they hit us! Bring the fight to them and kill them quick!" Venom added slamming his fist down on the table.

It didn't take long for the pair of sergeants to leave for the search. They both got in the van and drove off. It never occurred to Red that if this mission was a failure and both died that the Vipers would have to continue without the two best members of their team, their sergeant and the legendary Venom. He knew that they were both sent in because the current mission needed the best. Venom, who was driving turned slightly to Red who was in the back fixing together a sniper rifle.

"So then Red, do you have any idea how we are supposed to know where the masters domain is?"

"Well, no, I just thought our intelligence found that out"

Venom tutted

"No, not at all. They don't have a clue, most of us guys ever do and yet this time, miraculous ...I do"

"How?" Red asked. Venom either didn't hear him or pretended not to, as he kept driving and said nothing so Instead Red asked a totally different question   "How many vampires are there in this intelligence group?"

"I'll do more than just tell you how many, I'll tell you their names... Victor Van Vamp, Tanya Van Vonya and their daughter Sasha Vamp, they are a family, not just some random group that was thrown together"

"How can you know that?" Red asked

"Lets just say, I had a little run in with them a long time ago, things didn't go so well, they will this time"

The van stopped and Venom got out almost instantly slamming the door behind him, seconds later the side door opened showing Red who unlike Venom wasn't wearing any black or hood.

"Why do you insist on not wearing uniform?" Venom asked

"Because I want to be different." Red answered with a snort of laughter

"Ah well, you've already achieved that title" They both stood in the road looking into a lifeless, dull, grey sky

"This is it" Said Venom pointing at a tall tower behind them which shared the same grey gloom as the atmosphere.

"Well, I wasn't expecting a five star hotel" Red said following Venom to the doors

"Remember, these vampires are very skilled, the best of the best, they've been training for years. When we go in there, there will be no talking, we will be silent as shadow, signs and hand signals only" Venom said before entering the building.

The pair of Viper's were surprised to see it was almost like a sewage system, huge, snake like drains winded through the corridors hanging high above them, It was a good thing the double knew a little bit of sign language because the slightest bit of noise could have been magnified by the echoes of the tunnels. Dirty, brown, stinking water travelled down the middle of the two gang ways. The sergeants walked cautiously along the edge of the walkway staring in disgust into the rat infested waters. They held their noises tight and moved through the dark, dank, disgraceful sewers until reaching a junction which split up into two separate directions. They looked at each other, Red raising an eyebrow. Venom listened then pointed down the one ahead of them, Red nodded then they continued. A well spoken voice echoed down the sewers soon after which forced them both to a startled halt but after checking the tunnels around them they carried on, this time following the voice.

"The master died a vampire faithful to his clan. He was also faithful to god even though it was exactly that that killed him in the first place. We may not share his beliefs but we will respect his ways and give him a proper funeral. Now...ARRRR! Well that is his arm off. And now...ARRR!! Oh damn, I have done it wrong, the leg was supposed to come off first. Oh well, now for the head...1...2...3...oh crap! You stupid RATS! Arrr, darling get rid of those god damn rats will you?" After that it was quiet again.

The voice led them to a small air vent half way up the next tunnel. They stopped Venom pointed to himself showing one finger then to Red showing two fingers. Red nodded then got out a small knife. Slowly he unscrewed the four screws around the sides of the vent. He carefully placed each screw down on the floor then finally the air vent cover. With a nod the two Vipers climbed in and began crawling up the narrow almost crushing vent. If he didn't have to be so quiet Venom would have burst out laughing, how ridiculous the pair of them must have looked to anyone else, they obviously hadn't the faintest clue how to behave like proper spies or whatever you would call them, Venom realised now after so many long years working for the Viper's that they were just some big joke, they had no idea what they were doing and yet, blindly stumbling along they managed to get stuff done and still they hadn't ever been completely wiped out... but how long could that last?

Somewhere deep within the maze of filthy tunnels there stood two vampires. One, a male with ginger cropped hair and a grey dusty suit, and the other one, a female with long, black hair tied back into a ponytail with two long tresses that ran down her face, she wore a long coat with tails which brushed the floor around the corpse. Victor, the ginger haired vampire held an axe drenched in blood, little did they know that they were being watched by two Vipers one who was aiming a sniper rifle right at them

"Ok, kill Victor first, from what I've heard he should be the bigger threat" Whispered Venom out the side of his mouth. Red took a long, deep breath then got ready to fire, just as he was about to pull the trigger a voice from behind them echoed making him jump out of his skin.

"You're the biggest pair of rats I've ever seen!"

Chapter three: Be head

"Shit!!" Yelled Red firing a shot at the ceiling by mistake. Venom span around pulling out a pistol, he aimed it at the girl, eyeing her features cautiously, black hair, eyeliner, red jumper, purple mini skirt, huge, rose red lips.

"Sorry to do this Sasha" He said before blasting a hole in her chest. She fell backwards gasping.

"You bastard!" She cursed more from annoyance then pain, pulling out the bullet with both sets of black claws. Venom aimed again, this time at her head.

"I've been sent to kill you" Venom said

"No such luck!" Cried Victor who knocked into his back sending him flying, the gun went off but missed its target completely, pinning into Sasha's arm instead. Victor landed on top of Venom swinging the bloody axe over his head towards Venom's neck he quickly knocked it away with his hand slicing off his two middle fingers in the process. Victor prepared another chop then collapsed backwards yelling in pain, Red stood behind him holding the gun to his head.

"Die vampire!"

"Make me!" Replied Victor disappearing before his eyes

"Oh damn!" Shouted Red twisting around looking for him, Victor's invisible fist pounded into his face, Red slammed against the wall of the underground hall then he froze; his neck tightening as the invisible Victor clutched it.

"Don't point that thing at me!" He snarled.

201

Venom rushed towards his comrade coming to his aid but Tanya jumped between them

"Your friend is going to die, you can't save him now. Just leave here!" She warned.

He carefully aimed his gun down making it look like he was going to place it down then fired, the shot struck Tanya's foot and she crashed to the floor Venom ran ahead but fell short of his target; Tanya grabbing his ankle.

"Get off me Tanya!" He roared, kicking out at her. "I'm only leaving here with my friend alive!"

Tanya ignored his pleas and instead injected her nails into his bone "God Damn it woman!! Get off of me!" He shouted writhing in agony, watching helplessly as sergeant Red struggled with Victor, Red's eyes bulged and he dropped his sniper rifle to claw at his neck. The gun crashed to the floor sending an ear ringing shot at Victor's face, his face lit up as the shot drilled into his skull, he dropped to the floor instantly without time to scream or yell, his axe clinking against the ground.

Everyone fell silent then Red started to cough, grabbing his throat as he recovered. Tanya let go of Venom instantly, getting up and moving like an athlete towards Victor's body, Venom reached out to grab her but a pain erupted from his foot as a steel blade sliced against it.

"ARR!!" He thundered, dropping to one knee, turning to face a recuperated Sasha. Tanya raced to Red snatching up the axe from the blood spilt floor. Everything seemed to move in slow motion as Venom cried a warning to Red, as Tanya swung for his head, as Red turned and the axe collided with his neck biting through it like an enraged wolf, as Red felt his life spilling out, as he let out a quick horrified yelp, as his head rolled off and onto the floor. Blood dribbled from his neck and soaked Tanya's bare feet as she kneeled at Victor's body, blood and tears dripping from her face onto him.

"Victor?!" She screamed, there was no reply. The shot must have blown through his brain. Tanya stood up slowly, emotionlessly, swaying like a zombie, then she turned to Venom showing her distraught, furious face. Her eyes were burning with sadness and anger, covered in tears. Her lips quivered madly.

"You!" She said, pointing at Venom. "I told you to leave! Why did you not listen? Why didn't you leave us alone? We haven't done anything to you!" She cried.

"It is my job!"

"What?! To make our lives a misery?! You sadistic freak! We told you before, you know nothing about us vampires" She whimpered.

"You're the monsters! You need to be locked up" With those last words Venom shuddered, a chill running down his back, it reminded him of something he thought about someone else a long time ago.

"Don't say that" He whispered. "You killed one of mine, you've had your revenge"

Tanya shook her head. "NO, no we haven't, we've only just begun!" At that she looked past Venom at Sasha.

"Kill him!" Sasha didn't even say anything, she just simply ran towards him wielding a jagged, round, rusted blade saw. Tanya ran from the other side still holding her axe high above her head, just as Venom was about to get ripped to pieces by the pair of vampires, the wall from behind him exploded forcing him to dive to the ground covering his face with his arms for barriers. Rubble crashed down around him. Sasha and Tanya fell also, scampering away from the falling debris.

Venom looked up and spotted Rodlack who stood on the other side of the hall with a huge rocket launcher jammed to his shoulder "Come on Venom! Get out of there!!" He ordered beckoning to him. The old Viper got up then ran past his comrades headless body accidentally kicking his head across the room the blood smearing up his black trousers, he reached Rodlack who was continuously letting off rockets at the fleeing vampires.
"Let's go... maybe?" Venom suggested. Rodlack threw his rocket launcher down and turned to Venom "Just one more thing" He pulled out a small round ball. A time bomb! That should wipe out these scum!" He Cheered lobbing it before escaping with Venom to the helicopter still hanging in midair.
"Go, go, go!!" Demanded Venom to the pilot before jumping out of the smashed in wall along with Rodlack. They both landed awkwardly with no time to get up they watched the tower explode in a burst of amazing power and come crumbling down.

Chapter four: The boy is back in town

"Leave me alone!" The horrified woman cried rushing down the alleyway. She hit a dead end and burst into tears. She turned and looked into the swallowing darkness

"I'm still here" Called a voice from within the shadows

"Stop following me! What have I done to you?" The woman cried laying back against the soaking wall, the rain poured down around her drenching her clothes making her shiver wildly her teeth chattering uncontrollably.

"Why are you here?!" She asked

"Because your beautiful eyes led me astray, I can't help it, your so lovely" Purred the voice.

"Leave me alone! I'm scared and cold and just want to go home!" She pleaded

"No way"

The woman's eyes searched the shadows frantically, her heartbeat pounding against her chest, threatening to burst through her ribcage

"Don't do this! Please! I'm begging you!"

"Ohhhh yes, beg, beg. That's right... the more you beg the more you arouse my passion for the kill"

"Leave me!! I just want to go home!"

Everything went silent

"Hello?" Whimpered the woman "Are you there?" A hand of relief gripped her as her heart rate started to grow slower again. All that happened after that was a chorus of screams as Thomas Darkne appeared directly in front of her face, he bit into her nose, latching on to her. He silenced her with a quick snap, he twisted her nose to the side before tearing it away from her, her bones jutted out like broken splints. Darkne kneeled at her body and stroked her frozen, cold back.

"Nothing wrong with a bit of frozen flesh" He said before ripping free another huge chunk.

The Vipers helicopter soared over the city.

"So, what happened to Red?" Asked Rodlack

"He got beheaded"

"Ok… well, looks like you'll be back in control of our base. Just like old times eh?"

"Hopefully not" Answered Venom remembering the sadistic voice of Thomas Darkne

"Now that the Vamp's are dealt with what do we do?" Asked Rodlack

"Well, we just hack a few police lines and listen out for Vampiric activities" The sarge said. "What we… erm… normally do"

Soon later the helicopter landed outside the Vipers secret base. This one wasn't as flash as the first base Venom had been in. No underwater windows or steel corridors, no secret rooms which only he had access to. This one was simple, just an old, abandoned warehouse. Some of the rooms were added on and placed underground but not many. There was a ladder leading up to a walkway which aligned the windows high up above and stretched all the way around the room, so Vipers could be up there on the look out (Which of course they never needed to do). Venom, Rodlack and Vick the pilot barged in through the large double doors. Venom alerted his workers with…

"So then, have we found anything of use?"

"No sir, not as yet sir" Said Venox standing up from his computer, he was always a bit of a suck up.

"Well, Vipers. We have some bad news to tell you" Venom begun, everyone stopped working and fell silent listening to their unofficial leader.

"Red is dead" He announced. No one moved, even though they had already noticed Red was missing before Venom started to talk they weren't expecting this, it hit them all equally as hard as it would if they had heard of a relatives death.

"Now I know this is some shocking news and believe me it'll take even me a little while to get my head around it but that is not an excuse to stop working" He added, forgetting how most people reacted to death, they weren't all as used to it as him. "Go on! Work!!" He ordered, they all gradually, slowly turned back to their computer screens and continued working, this time without talking amongst each other.

"Rodlack, Vick. Come with me" Venom said before leading them to the next room, this room was dark, and empty, a cold air filled the atmosphere. Venom lit some candles then spoke. "Do we have any females working for us?"

"No" Answered Rodlack. "Why?"

"Because I am the sergeant once again, I'm allowed to ask questions aren't I?! If someone wanted to break in here then could we lock them out?"

"Ermm, not really sir"

"Well that's not very good is it?"

"Ermm, no sir" Said Rodlack. Sergeant Venom didn't say anything else, he just stared at something on the floor.

"Sir?" Called Vick "What's wrong?"

Venom picked up a small piece of paper from the floor. It had red writing spread out across it in letter form.

"Where did that come from sir?" Asked Rodlack, Venom looked at them about to ask what business it was of his but then he sighed, his mind elsewhere completely

"I don't know, it was just there, on the floor, who could have left it there?" Asked Venom

"Why don't you just read it?" Asked Vick, Venom went back to staring at the piece of paper.

"Because I think I know who it's from" Answered Venom in deep thought, he unfolded the paper and read it to himself.

HELLO, MY OLD FRIEND. I BELIEVE YOU KNOW WHO I
AM. I AM BACK FROM MY HOLIDAY AND I AM NOW
ALSO BACK IN TOWN. ALREADY I AM BACK ON MY
KILLING SPREE BUT THINGS JUST DON'T FEEL THE SAME
WITHOUT YOU. I WOULD LIKE TO SEE YOU AGAIN
AND I KNOW YOU WOULD LIKE TO SEE ME AGAIN TOO
SO I WILL BE WAITING FOR YOU SOMEWHERE. I THINK
YOU CAN FIND ME WITHOUT HAVING DIRECTIONS.
I'LL TEST YOU. CAN YOU FIND ME? IF YOU TURN UP AT
THIS PLACE AT ONE O'CLOCK IN THE MORNING
THEN... WELL I WILL BE WAITING FOR YOU THERE.
GOOD LUCK SARGEY WARGEY

ALL MY LOVE

THOMAS. D

Sergeant Venom looked up, an expression torn between demented
relief and sickening fear.
"Damn! He's bloody well back!"

Chapter five: The date

"Ok, I'm meeting up with an old friend of mine. I need some snipers to come with me. We need to take this vampire down!"

"Wait, you want to kill him?"

"He's a vampire!"

"But you just said he was an old friend"

"Yes, an old friend who must die" Said the sarge

"I can't just kill anyone you tell me to" Replied Vick.

"Well of course you can... I'm your sergeant"

"Can you tell us who this is?" Asked Rodlack.

"You wouldn't believe me if you tried"

"You may be the sergeant but your really beginning to piss me off!" Shouted Vick

"OK! He's a magician-"

"A... magician? We hunt vampires, not magicians" Said Rodlack

"Don't you know what a magician is?" Asked Venom grabbing Rodlack by the collar of his shirt

"Well, a magic man? Sir?"

"Like vampires only worse, more powerful. Humans with magical abilities, this particular one is hell to deal with"

"Explain yourself!" Yelled Vick. "You obviously haven't just been hanging around with this guy, how do you know him? Tell us now!" He demanded.

The Sarge put Rodlack down and sat in a small wooden chair away from the light of the candles.

"I suppose I should explain everything." He let out a long sigh then continued.

"This magician is called Thomas Darkne. We had trouble realising he was of human origin at first, we thought he was a vampire-" The sarge was interrupted by the impatient Vick

"Who's we?"

"The group of Viper's I was with before. We hunted him down thinking he was a vampire. We were wrong, he was a cannibal, a murdering maniac, he ate women and killed for sport, for fun. Everyday we would find one women dead, half eaten and a man half recognisable. He said he killed one for food, one for play, then anyone else who got in his way. He also killed Blake, probably the best Viper I've ever known, then the murderer attacked our highly secured base, he managed to brainwash a fellow Viper who was inside and he let himself in using the Viper as a puppet. He killed everyone inside, he killed Scar then he flooded the base trapping me inside a vault with him." He paused for a second lost in his haunting memories

"There he said he would keep me alive, he didn't say why, when I asked how I was going to escape, he didn't say, he just knew I would. During our chat he sent me some kind of telepathic message, I can't explain it but just as I was about to blast a bullet through my head I got the message, it told me exactly who he was, how I was going to get out of the base alive. He showed me the way. He also gave me a number-" He left out the bit about him accidentally absorbing some of Darkne's power though.

"Right, so that's how you wound up here" Said Rodlack

"What number?" Quizzed Vick

"I couldn't possibly tell you that" Said the Sarge almost immediately looking up at them, fear swelling in his face

"Reds number? That's how he found you? I knew it wasn't just skill!"

"NO!" Thundered Venom shutting them both up. "That's what I don't understand. I didn't talk to anyone on the phone, the phone rang six times then someone picked up but there was only silence. I listened, hoping someone would talk... then I almost died on the spot... Someone screamed, a chorus of screams, seeming to be from more then one mouth! In agony, terrible agony... cursing me, telling me it was all my fault" He shuddered "You know what? You don't need to know all this, I've told you what you need, now as my men, you do as you're told" He set his eyes on them with an intimidating stare and they didn't argue any more.

The Sergeant stood, peering around at the abandoned street, huge chunks of rubble lying around him, smashed buildings either side of him with windows blown out, doors battered down, wooden splinters in masses on the floor. It was obvious to Venom why Darkne had chosen this spot, no one around; no one would be coming here. It was emptied ages ago for demolishing and they never got round to finishing the job. To Venoms right, one of the top windows was covered by as sniper, hidden in the shadows. Venom couldn't see any of the snipers but he knew where they were. One directly behind him in the far building with a roof that had fallen in years ago, one watching from in front, every few minutes Venom could see the metal from the gun glint in the dim sunlight. He didn't feel much comfort knowing they were there however as he wasn't so sure that Darkne would fall for his trap but it was his only hope.

"Hello Venom" Came the dreadful voice, Venom jumped.

"DARKNE!? Where are you?"

"Here" He said appearing before his eyes like a hologram. "I haven't seen you for a long time" He said. "Nice to see you again."

"I can't say the same for you" Replied Venom eyes quickly snapping to the sniper in the window over Darkne's shoulder

"Why Darkne, why?" He asked, the questions burst free from his dam like lips

"Why what Sarge?"

"Why did you help me escape? Why did you give me that number? Why am I still alive?" The questions came spilling out

"A number you say? I don't remember giving you a number" He snarled, thinking back, a finger resting on his lips

"6 6!" Venom roared

"Well, that's not a number is it? That's quite obviously two numbers"

"Well yes, but-"

Thomas interrupted again

"As for you being alive, I hope to end that!" He growled stepping forward quickly, grabbing Venoms cowl neck tight, he lurched

213

forward, opening his mouth, his razor like teeth hanging an inch away from the jelly on his eye!

Chapter Six: Suck on this!

Venom's eyes were firmly shut; he felt the end of his life closing down around him. He could feel the cannibal's hot, stinking breath on his face. Then Darkne withdrew his head slightly and Venom slowly opened his eyes again. It seemed to Venom that the murderer was merely staring into his eye, not trying to steal it away from him
"Keep your eyes open!" Darkne ordered, pulling the eyelids apart until he could see the red veins bulging out from the sockets. Venom could see the sniper over Darkne's shoulder preparing to take a shot at his head. Then, in a flash, the thought came to Venom, Thomas could see him too! Too late to stop it now, Darkne smiled his sarcastic, gruesome smile then said.
"Naughty boys!" Swinging the Sergeant over his shoulder and smashing him to the ground he span around, his head coming into the snipers sight centre.

The sniper Viper tightened his grip around the trigger and **his** head exploded, in a blood burst, blood shot into the air around his head, which now remained on the floor in a huge circle of pink, stripes of flesh, which still wriggled for life. The Vipers body slammed down to the ground, crushing segments of his brain. Darkne turned to the Sergeant who was laying on the ground clutching his knee
"One down, two more to go" Cheered Darkne. Two bullets zipped through the air towards him but they disintegrated in seconds. Thomas span around looking in the top window of a building

215

"Hello!" He shouted he then clicked his fingers and the roof collapsed, falling in on the sniper, the rest of the building fell in on itself turning into a heap of bricks and dust

"Now for you!" Darkne said looking at the last Viper sniper. He wiggled his finger towards him, beckoning him forward; the Viper froze, dropped his gun then started to levitate through the air towards the dark master.

"Come boy" Darkne demanded, the Viper landed by his side still unable to move

"Sit boy" Shouted Darkne, the Viper zombie kneeled at his feet.

"Thank you, now…" Darkne's eyes lit up as he leant forward towards the Vipers neck,

"Feed boy!!" Darkne bit into the Vipers neck, Venom watched, fear stricken on the floor as his comrades neck snapped. As Darkne set his teeth around something he lifted his hand and made an 'ok' sign. Thomas jerked backwards sending a spray of blood flying at Venom's face. Darkne turned, a thin, cylinder shape in between his teeth, the mans gullet! Darkne spat it at Venom.

"You know I don't eat the males, he's still alive, but barely… lets hear him scream" Darkne said clicking his fingers. The Viper burst into action slapping his hands at the jagged hole in his neck; his screams were tightened, more like a pathetic squeal of a pig. Blood was shooting from his wound rapidly and there was no stopping until he just twitched wildly before falling to the floor in a puddle of his own fluid.

Venom stood up shakily and walked over to Darkne looking at his red chin.

"You might want to wipe that up" He said trying to sound unaffected.

"Do correct me if I'm wrong but people can't scream when their gullets are missing can they?" He added.

"Well done! No they cannot, but I'm very good at these things. I ripped someone's head off without killing them once" Said Darkne smiling widely.

"Wow, what an achievement"

Thomas wiped his chin with his hand then flicked it at Venom.

"So, do you not care that these people are dead?" Asked Darkne, intrigued.

"No, no I don't care. To be totally honest... I -" Venom stopped to gulp. "You've killed so many people in my life I don't care anymore"

"OH!" Shrieked Darkne. "You've really hurt my feelings now" He said stepping towards Venom. He stuck out his hand showing Venom his bony, long, red nailed fingers

"Take my hand Venom, trust me"

"Why?" Venom stared down

"Trust me!"

Venom reached down and touched his hand, not wanting to make too much contact. Darkne grabbed his hand tight squeezing down on his fingers; Venom flinched but didn't fight back. Thomas Darkne started to talk.

"Do they feel like a cold blooded murderer's?"

"NO, they're warm, really warm" Answered Venom trying to keep on

217

Darkne's better side.

"Thank you" Said Darkne rubbing Venoms vein that ran up from his palm to the end of his arm. In an instant Darkne pulled Venoms hand up to his jaws, he shoved the fingers in and bit down saying out of the corner of his mouth.

"What about NOW!? Do I feel like a cold blooded killer now?" Blood was pouring down Venoms arm, his hand already drenched in the liquid. Thomas bared his teeth getting a better grip around his two middle fingers. (This was the opposite hand to the one with the already missing middle fingers) With one crunch Venoms fingers disappeared down Darkne's throat. Blood flowed out of Darkne's mouth freely as Venoms hand shoot across in the air back to Venoms side.

"Sorry Darkne but your time is up" Hissed Venom through gritted teeth. Darkne twisted around to see a group of hooded men wielding machine guns. One of them stood to one side and ordered them forward

"Protect the Sarge! KILL THE FREAK!!" The men aimed at Darkne. Thomas smiled, looking at the Vipers then he disappeared, gone!! Venom cursed then dropped to the floor, blood still gushing out from his missing fingers. The gun wielding Vipers stopped, Rodlack pulling down his hood

"DAMN!"

☐

Chapter seven: Under the sea

It had been weeks since. None of the Vipers had heard about any murders sounding even remotely as if they belonged to Darkne since that day, except Venom. This was because every death record that came through describing a half eaten body on the Vipers monitors was secretly blocked and only Venom's personal monitor could access them. So as everyone was celebrating the fact that no more gruesome deaths had occurred Venom was going insane at the fact that the deaths had in fact multiplied, turning from one as food and one as fun to one for food and nine for fun. The Sarge's brain was being tortured and ripped apart by an invisible demon of sadness, guilt and agony. He wasn't allowed to show any of his true emotions to the other Vipers or else they would know something was wrong, so the sergeant disguised himself with lies all the time until he thought of something which he was shocked and amazed at by the fact that he had never thought of it before.

His old base! It had the secret room. In that room there was something hidden inside a safe something very unique held in it. Something that could never be found anywhere else in this world, a device with the ability to destroy Darkne once and for all. If that safe was still there and hadn't been ruined then he could go and collect it from the bottom of the sea! But first Venom knew he had to convince some others to go with him. Rodlack, Vick and Venox. They would be his targets. From his dark room in his wooden chair he leaned over and pressed down the red button which triggered telecoms. Like a staff announcement in a supermarket, his voice rang out "RODLACK, VICK, COME TO MY ROOM NOW!" Venom waited for a few moments and then stood near the door. Rodlack burst through the door, followed by Vick

"What is it now Sarge? What are you hiding from us this time?"

"Well, I have a confession to make"

"Yes, it didn't take a genius to know that, what is it?" Asked Vick

"I jammed your computers and headsets so that the cannibal murders wouldn't show up and you would know nothing about him" Venom explained.

"I knew it! I knew he didn't just disappear from the area... why?" Asked Vick suspiciously.

"Because, I know we can't stop him. If we go after him he'll only kill more of us. But now I know of something that will rip him apart!" Answered the Sarge excitedly

"We can get rid of him?" Questioned Rodlack unconvinced

"Yes! It's so simple I'm amazed I didn't think of it before"

"So where is this, something?" Asked Rodlack

"Under the sea. My old base had a secret room which tunnelled under the seabed, it had a strong, almost unbreakable seal on It. The water might not have got in!"

"This is going to work?" Quizzed Rodlack

"Only if you are going to make it work, you're with me or you're fired. You and Vick and two of your best men go down to retrieve the 'Something' Tonight!"

Back at the site of the old Viper base Venom stood at the edge of the water, his feet where the front gatehouse would have been, still, there were thin bits of metal jutting out of the ground around his boots, so many memories were rushing back to Venom as he stared out at the vast, blue sea where his base was drowned. Venom, Rodlack, Vick and two of their best men in the group, Venoz and Zemos, two brothers, all of them were clothed with diving suits, yellow helmets covering their heads giving them the look of space men from a small children's book.

"Let's go down, follow me and steer clear of broken metal and glass from the base. I don't think anyone's cleared it yet, which is better for us as it means they haven't tampered with anything" Ordered Venom, one look around at each other was all they needed before diving into the water. Sergeant Venom cleared his visor then stared down at the sea bed. He pointed his men downwards and they descended.

Venom soon uncovered the seal; it was a good job the sea wasn't too deep here. Venom called them down then searched the seal for an opening. He ran his fingers around the sides then pushed down with his next hand. The seal opened! The bunch of Vipers bundled in quickly and pushed the button down, closing the steel jaws before too much water got in. They stood around the room watching the Sarge lift a large safe from off the floor which was shallowly filled with water

"Ok people, this is what I've been hiding in this safe for years, never got it out after I put it there." Venom smiled turning the combination dial until it clicked. The door swung open. Venom gleefully put his hand in to grab the object held inside. Suddenly everyone froze! Their heads all turned as one as the seal in the ceiling began to open. The sergeants eyes widened

"DARKNE!" He cried. "He must be watching us!" The water spilled in through the hatch in a massively forceful rush. The seal wouldn't close again whilst the strong water was crashing through. The room filled almost instantly and the Vipers began to start losing head room, the water level quickly ascending up their chests

"I know what he's trying to do" Shouted Venom.

"He's trying to drown us!" Yelled Venox.

"No, we can't drown while we're wearing these suits. He's going to trap us down here by closing the seal once the room has filled then he will boil the water!" Shrieked Venom, the Vipers were too clouded with worry to ask why and how he knew that.

"So we're going to get cooked alive? Like in some giant, demonic oven?!" Screamed Rodlack, no one had a chance to answer as the water rose above their mouths.

Venom closed the safe door then swam towards the seal, racing for it, kicking his legs rapidly in order to reach it before it closed. He reached out his hand and almost got the rest of his fingers sliced off by the force of the seal closing. They were now trapped in the 'oven!' As Venom had foretold the water started to heat up!! Venom looked down upon his unfortunate group who started to scream silently as the water began to boil up, inside their suits they could feel their skin bubbling up and bursting, their muscles melting and reducing to scorching hot liquid. The Vipers opened up their mouths for the last time to let out one last agonised scream for life, Venom watched their heads explode with intense pressure knowing he would be next!

Chapter Eight: Samantha

D.S Samantha Slay walked down the white corridor approaching D.S Vein with a very serious look on her otherwise tender face.

"Is he okay?" She asked quickly

"He's in pretty bad shape, but your friend will be better soon, with our help"

"Good news and-" Samantha blinked. "Don't worry"

"Yes, you'll be in charge of that" Chuckled Vein

"In charge of what sir?" She asked with fake innocence

"Don't think I don't know what you want"

"Ok, well thank you. It's a very nice gift" She smiled before walking away looking very smug

"Erm... Sam!" Called Vein

"Yes sir?!" She answered spinning on her heels

"10210666" Said Vein

"Great" Laughed Sam happily, a sly smile flashing onto her face.

She arrived at the old warehouse walking up to the doors she knocked hard five times, she waited listening to the people on the other side.

"Who is it?" Called a voice

"D.S Samantha Slay, someone has sent me to see you"

"What does D.S stand for?"

"Don't worry, I'm not a police woman"

"And how do we know to trust you?" Quizzed the voice.

"10210666" Sam said, the door slowly swung open revealing a Viper on the other side

"Hello" Sam said as she saw him.

"What is it that you want?" Asked the Viper before letting her pass him.

"I want to know what you're doing" Sam answered simply.

"Like we'd tell you that"

"I know more then you think, you must trust me, I gave you that number!!" Sam shouted. Vipers around her didn't look convinced as they turned on their chairs, looking away from their computer screens.

"Ok" She sighed. "I know about Thomas Darkne" She finally burst out

"Oh... I see" Said the Viper staring at D.S Samantha Slay with concern. Her short, shining, red hair which barely brushed the epaulettes on her shoulders and flame design trousers, big, heavy looking, black boots looked suspicious to him. It meant she wasn't a member of any type of normal service. She seemed professional at whatever it was that she was doing and to make it worse, she knew some unwanted info about Thomas Darkne, something THEY were trying to keep secret.

"What do you know about him?" Asked the Viper.

"Not much, I know you've been tracking him for some time now, and that he's a very exceptional magician. Me and my friends know all about magic. What are you planning to do about this Darkne person?" Sam said, explaining herself.

"Well" Started the Viper giving up his unease. "Venom went off with four other to collect a special object that can kill him, he just told us to defend the base and look out for Darkne"

"Ok, good, well I'm here to warn you now that your base is going to need some defending very soon." Sam said

"What!"

"You are going to get attacked, very soon"

"By Darkne!!"

"I don't know" Began Samantha, she was interrupted by a worried Viper from behind her.

"Sir!" He cried, "Our cameras have just gone dead"

"Oh great!" Cursed the Viper. "OK, Zee, Xeonix, Franc. Get up to those windows!!" He ordered, taking control of the nerve-racking situation. The three appointed Vipers rushed to their positions and aimed their high power machine guns out of the windows, on look out, like crows.

"Okay, bar those doors!" Ordered their commanding Viper. A long bar of steel was lined up against the only escape or entrance

"Get your guns ready!" Warned the Viper, the next voice was Sam's

"Well I'd love to stay and help but I'm needed elsewhere… sorry" She then turned to the second door which led to Venoms darkroom

"But woman!! We might need your help!" Called the commander after her.

"Sorry" She replied by waving backwards at him.

"And… that's not the right way… oh, who cares!" Another Viper appeared before the commanders eyes

"Sir, I have found some information about Thomas Darkne's position"

He said excitedly. The commander snatched up the paper and read it quickly

"But... if Darkne's all the way out there, who's out there?" He asked, pointing at the door

"I haven't a clue sir"

The Vipers who were positioned on the windows turned to the commander.

"Sir, there's two of ours outside!!"

"Well... get them in god dammit!!" Yelled the commander urgently.

"Before that THING gets them!!"

The two Vipers strolled casually up to the warehouse door. The irritated voice of the Vipers called from out of the windows.

"Get inside! There's someone out there who may be a danger to us all!"

The pair of Vipers jumped into action rushing to the door immediately, their fists smashed against the metal as the Vipers on the other side scrabbled around with the slab that barred the door shut. One of the Vipers from outside screamed, the other turned to his companion, blood gushed from his throat drenching his neck and chin, a round, jagged disk with sharp teeth like points jammed to his gullet!

Chapter nine: You've been framed

The unharmed Viper ran past the door in a burst of worry giving up getting inside the barred gates, he ran around the corner of the building and into a narrow alleyway, he reached the back wall then collapsed with his back leaning against it. He pulled out his pistol and aimed it down the entrance of the alley. He was shivering with fear, he and his friend were new recruits. Sweat dripped down his brow as he watched a young teenage girl with long, black hair step around the corner holding a bloodied blade saw, she was smiling menacingly with her purple lips. The Viper went to pull the trigger when a white pale claw latched on to his arm from above, the Viper shrieked as his arm was twisted and broken in seconds, his eyes wide with terror looking up at a grinning face, the Viper opened his mouth to yell but the monsters head shot down in a flash and tore through his face.

Back inside the Vipers base the Vipers were getting worried. "They're both dead, they've got to be" was all they could say or think, nervously reloading their guns for no reason over run with fear. "Pull yourselves together men! We've got a chance with this thing! One of them ten of us!" The commander shouted trying to raise spirits. "It's not Thomas Darkne! It can't be, he's somewhere completely different" A wave of relief washed over the crowd, one Viper who was standing nearby turned to him. "Why didn't you say so? Boys we've got nothing to worry about-" He was cut short as an ear ringing crash echoed through the room. All of the hooded heads peered upwards towards the weak, metal material ceiling; someone or something was banging against it! The men at the windows pointed their guns towards the shadow that was shown through the roof.

"Get ready boys!" Warned the commander "Fingers on triggers" The ceiling was smashed again, harder this time, then the third smash was from the left, the door fell to the floor the steel bars across it being useless of course, the unaware Viper nearest the door was knocked into by a ginger haired vampire, the Vipers arm dropped to the floor, cut clean off by the vampires sword, the vampire hunter fell to the ground crying in pain. The ceiling crashed open and a dark haired woman flew down through it on a zip line, she shot at the men below with a pistol, an axe in the other hand. One man fell dead, the others running away from her, she landed behind another who didn't have a chance to react, he was too busy watching the ginger vampire pin his sword through the Viper with no arm. The female vampire swung her axe around, the Vipers head rolling off. The surrounding vampire hunters turned to her ready to shoot when she turned invisible, one Viper cried out as a fist connected with his face his arms flailing as he fell backwards. The others shot blindly. The three at the window were looking out the glass at something, a red bleeping badge

"It's a bomb!" Bellowed one of them

"No" Purred a voice. "Just a distraction"

The trio spun round to see a teenage vampire holding a chainsaw at the other end of the hanging metal balcony where they stood.

"Feel like a free fall?" She asked before ramming her chainsaw between the wall and the latches that held it upright

"I've already done the other side boys don't you worry" She shouted over the light rumble of her specialised silenced chainsaw. The balcony dropped, the three Vipers yelping and trying to run before it broke loose. Sasha took flight then clung onto the wall with her sharp nails and high heels. Two Vipers fell to their deaths, two more crushed by the metal from above and the third Viper landed uneasily, breaking almost every bone in his body but he was still alive. Seconds later Sasha landed onto of his back, her saw slicing his head in half like a coconut.

"Oops" she said sarcastically as she stomped her boot through his brain splashing the fluid. The three vampires (the Vamps) surrounded the commander and the last standing Viper. They threw their guns down in surrender.

"Good job you did that" Said Victor walking ahead of Sasha and Tanya

"I thought you were dead!" Gasped the Commander

"That is all you could say to us?" Asked Victor. "We do not die too easily, we escaped of course, Red misplaced his lucky bullet just two centimetres away from my brain. We wanted revenge on all of you so called vampire slayers and now we are almost finished." Explained Victor.

"Almost?" Asked the second Viper

"You're not dead yet" Answered Tanya pointing at them.

"But... we've surrendered!" Cried the Commander

"That was stupid, we did not give you that option" Said Victor walking forward even more towards the second Viper.

"NO!" The Viper roared rushing for his gun, Victor made a big step forward and thrust his long sword out it collided with his ribcage and ripped him off his feet. The Viper dangled in midair, his body limp, his arms still reaching pathetically for his gun even though he was dead. The commander zoomed forward picking up his gun but as his arm flew back into firing position Sasha's chainsaw gently brushed against the end of his finger nail and from the force and speed and bite of the saw the whole arm of skin was peeled straight off like a glove. The Commanders teeth ground down so hard that his teeth exploded in his mouth. He crashed to the floor, the information of Darkne's whereabouts sliding out of his pocket. Tanya stood over him with her axe swinging in her hand loosely above his back. She smiled then whispered...

"Goodnight" before letting the axe go, it fell then sliced into his back silencing him for ever.

☐

☐

☐

Chapter ten: School time

Sam stepped through the doorway of the Vipers warehouse staring at the blood shed around her.

'What the hell happened here?' She asked herself. She spotted the piece of paper across the hall and started towards it. Dodging the bits of corpses she made it safely across to her destination. Reading it she placed it in her pocket.

"Well that's lucky, he'll be pleased"

"Who will?" Called a voice from behind her, she jumped, turning round very quickly

"Oh god!" It was her colleague Peterson at the door. "You scared me!" She gasped

"Did you do this?" He asked raising an eye brow casually at the massacre.

"No, of course not!" She said walking past him into the outside.

"What did you find?" Peterson asked following her to a black and red flame van.

"You'll have to wait" She climbed into the vans side door and sat down next to a man who was bent over in deep, silent thought, a hood covering his face. Another man sat opposite called Vein, just Vein. Peterson got in and sat the other side of Sam. Sam called to the driver and told him to stay there a few moments.

"I've got something to show you boys" She said feeling around in her pocket pulling out the piece of paper

"You'll be happy with this" She informed the hooded man, he looked over to the paper, still hidden by his hood. Sam read the writing out loud to them.

"Report squadron 109: report of a man with tall, spiky, black gelled hair with eyeliner, black also and lipstick, black, and black suit-"

"Get on with it!" Interrupted Peterson, we know it's Darkne.

"Hmmm, was spotted running into a school playground in New York, I'm guessing to them it was more obvious to find, they are normally pretty vague. You can find out right?" She asked the driver

"Yes" Was the reply. "I'm already on it"

"So, because Darkne can't really hide himself in a school full of kids; he'd stick out like a sore thumb, he is probably possessing one of the kids" Sam finished

"I'll try to locate at least what class he would be in, that's probably as far as I can go for the moment. I can't locate the child directly but that will still be of help, narrows it down anyway." Said Vein placing his fingers on his temples and closing his eyes. Everyone spoke in hushed tones after that.

"Possessing an innocent child, I feared that he would think of that... why not just possess a teacher?" Said Peterson.

"Because" Began the hooded man. "He's too evil to pick a teacher, a teacher is less innocent then a small, baby face child."

"I couldn't kill a child" Whispered Peterson shaking his head

"Neither could I" Agreed Sam.

"Exactly, another reason why he picked a child" Said the mysterious man. Sam sat up trying to see into the boot of the van

"Have we got the gun?" She asked eagerly. "I can't wait to blow that Darkne to pieces once we get him out of the child's body" She said with an evil hiss.

"How come you get to operate that thing and I don't?" Asked Peterson like a jealous school boy.

"One, because I won't miss, two because we can only use it once and three because I look sexy in the power amour." Answered Sam. At that the hooded man stood up and walked to the very back of the van where he picked up a large, heavy, metallic gun. It was bigger in width of his waist and half the size in height of Sam. A wide cylinder shape nozzle was on the firing end, almost as big as a pint glass

"This baby will blow that mother to pieces!" Cheered Sam staring in amazement at its massive, chunky body work. "Thank you for keeping it safe" She added looking up at the man. He carefully placed it in her hands and sat down.

"So... Venom, how did you come across it?" Peterson asked the hooded man.

Actually Venom thought... how had he found it?

"I just found it buried in the sand on a beach somewhere next to a pub" He explained. "I did my research and soon began to realise its true purpose"

"Weird" Replied Peterson with an obvious tone of disappointment, nothing else was said after that. The van stopped and they got out the side door then crowded around on the pavement outside the school gates. Vein who was now out of his meditation was giving the orders

"Have the van ready, leave the doors open" He was shouting over the traffic around him filling the roads.

"We'll meet the rest of the team here then surround the school making sure all exits are securely covered, Sam at the main entrance, we'll try and chase him to her where she'll let loose a burst of power too big for even Darkne to deal with." Planned Vein.

Another van pulled up behind the first and unloaded even more men then the one before. They waited together on the pavement as Vein glared around at them.

"Venom, Peterson, Scorpon" He called, the three looked up from their spread out positions.

"You three go inside as… classroom inspectors, one pistol per person. Keep your weapons concealed; keep your eyes peeled for 'weirdness' and movement amongst the class. One of those students is possessed by Darkne, you must target and kill that student" He demanded. The three men who had grouped together while Vein spoke looked at him grimacing

"I will kill the child" Said Venom, knowing he was the one chosen for the job, he frowned, looking at the pistol in the inside pocket of his jacket.

"Are you sure?" Asked Peterson

"Darkne wouldn't have it any other way"

"GO!" Shouted Vein pointing through the school gates, the trio started out towards the main doors of the school.

"Ok Sam, get to your position" Vein shouted next, "We're counting on you" his voice faded into the distance.

The three men stopped at the doors, hiding their pistols within their clothes.

"Ok" Whispered Venom looking grimly at the other two. "This wont be easy, we wont pull this off without it resulting in many many innocent's deaths, we are just going to have to live with that" Venom rested his hand on the door handle.

"That's a fact"

Chapter eleven: Lesson time

Scorpon approached a member of staff outside a series of classroom doors in the long, narrow hall way

"Erm, hello, we are supposed to be inspecting a class of pupils today. Could we see room... 6 now please?" He lied

"I don't remember us inviting any inspectors for today... where's your identification?" The teacher asked looking at them uncertainly

"Oh I hate it when they do this" Cursed Scorpon turning to his team

"Excuse me?" Asked the bemused teacher from behind him.

Scorpon tutted then shook his head slowly. The teacher behind him fell to the floor with a loud thud.

"What happened?" Venom gasped

"She's out... for now, when she wakes up; which should be pretty soon she will have forgotten everything within the last hour" Explained Peterson.

"Oh good!" Exclaimed Venom suddenly void of any concern. "Is everyone with you a D.S?" He added

"Yes... we all have the ability to use or access at least a small amount of magical energy" Said Scorpon walking over to the teachers body then lead the rest of the group up the hall. They stopped at a green door with a small, square, glass window set in the top half of the wood. The translucent sheet that was laid across the glass made it almost impossible to see through only blurred images were made out. Venom opened the door interrupting the class and the teacher in mid speech

"Hello" Scorpon greeted awkwardly from behind Venom.

"Hello" Replied the male teacher. "And who would you sir's be?"

"We are the inspectors for today"

"Oh, ok"

"We checked in with the lady outside, now... we'll just take our seats and watch, no further disturbance will be made" Informed Scorpon.

"Ah yes, well please continue." said the teacher politely. Venom closed the door behind them then headed to a seat diagonal from the door giving him a full range of fire if Darkne tried to escape. Venom cast an eye around the class as he walked trying to pick up any small clues that might help him decide who Darkne's target was. No one in the class stuck out, they all stared at him with wide eyes all seeming identical to him.

Venom took his seat. Peterson sat opposite the door along the other wall next to the teachers' desk, Scorpon sat across from the door in the third corner. Venom's eyes shot around the room like darts trying to spot anything weird and out of place. The teacher's stern voice sounded almost silent and distant to him as he scored the room. Something caught his eye! He pinned his pupils to the spot, one child sitting across the table from another student slightly apart from the rest of the room. 'Good friends?' Thought the Sergeant. Scorpon was also keeping an eye on them, him being almost next to their table. The two boys didn't seem to be talking at that moment just staring lifelessly at the pencils on their desk. The boy opposite the other had an odd twitch, very distinct. Venom watched his movements closely, watching the small boys lips moving fast, as if talking to himself, Venom wondered if Scorpon could hear what he was saying. All of a sudden the nervous boy shot into action, standing up pushing his chair into the path of Scorpon. The young boy screamed rushing to the door, a set of keys appeared in his hand and he locked the door quickly.

"You're all going to die!" He yelled at the rest of the class, Peterson and Scorpon ran to him telling the other students to get down, the teacher dropped to the floor almost straight away, the other children slowly, unsurely ducked under their tables taking cover.

"You're all going to die!" The boy puppet continued to yell. Venom stood up then got out his gun running towards his target, he past the tables then shot; the bullet landing between the boy's eyes, right in the forehead, the boy collapsed, the room fell silent.

All three men had their guns pointing at the boy's body waiting for Darkne to appear before them, leaving his body... but nothing happened! The teacher stood up looking in shock at the dead boy then with a quivering voice shrieked.

"What on earth are you doing?!"

"Why isn't it working?" Questioned Peterson perplexed

"Darkne should be forced to leave the body!" Shouted Scorpon obviously as confused as the rest.

"I don't understand" Agreed Venom

"It's because it wasn't the right boy" Hissed an all too familiar voice from behind them, directly behind Venom, all three span around aiming their guns at another boy, it was the one who was sitting opposite.

"You unfortunately killed an innocent bystander" Said the boy shaking his head adopting the voice of Darkne

"Shoot me if you want, you can't kill me with bullets."

The boy's arms reached for his neck and tugged at the skin. His body ripped downwards in the middle like a zip, his flesh falling away from him like a thin layered, bloody coat smeared with organs of course. Then Thomas Darkne's form stepped over the pile of skin then stood smiling at the three terrified men

"I used my shell to whisper things to the other unfortunate boy sitting opposite me. Horrible things I said to him. Terrible things, I tortured his small, puny little child mind and twisted it inside out until he broke. I handed him the keys to the door and told him what he needed to do to stop me eating the jelly from his eyes. You killed a red herring Venom... just a herring!" Spat Darkne as he reached for him, an outstretched scarred, evil hand full of blades.

☐

☐

☐

Chapter Twelve: Lunch time!

An array of bullets blasted into Darkne's arm which pulled away in a flash.

"I said you'll have to do better then that, bullets don't hurt me. Be a bit more creative will you?" He said pulling loose the bullets one by one and dropping them to the floor. Scorpon's hand began to glow a pale purple, growing in colour and size as he held the pistol towards Darkne the metal also began to change colour and shook rapidly.

"Step back" Scorpon warned before pressing down on the trigger, an explosion of blinding light flashed through the room and a single shot rang out, the bullet surrounded by purple flames. It drilled into the targets forehead, the light dimmed just in time for Darkne to hiss in pain and in shock. He wiped a trail of blood off his head and flicked it to the ground

"Good, but you've got to play more dirty" Praised Darkne rushing as a blur towards Scorpon and before the magician knew what was happening the dark master was right in front of him.

"This is real dark magic" Said Darkne before thrusting his fist towards his chest, the whole room expected the hit to knock Scorpon flying but when he just stood there not moving at all they realised Darkne wasn't going for the skin or muscle but something deep beneath all that, his fist had torn right through the poor mans body, Venom and Peterson watched Thomas wave at them under the skin of Scorpon's back before his hand reappeared holding a pinkish rib bone.

Scorpon's lifeless shell fell like a dummy. Venom jumped to the side as Peterson shot out a small ball of purple light, it collided with Darkne's stomach and he was dragged back slightly gritting his teeth.

"Well this is definitely a fight isn't it? A poor fight but a fight none the less" Snarled Darkne waving a hand at Peterson, his muscles froze but only for a few seconds

"Very good Peter" Darkne clapped. "Allow me to explain sir Petersons actions" Talking to Venom now. "He knows I like to make muscles useless and use the muscle binding spells a lot so he has created a spell that sends a liquid around his body that flares up whenever my spell is activated which allows him to cope even with my spell in action. The flare is hot enough to burn away the spell but not boil himself alive... most useful, however I am very good at bending the rules of such spells" He grinned like a sly fox. "Let's turn the heat up a bit!"

Petersons eyes widened.

"Oh Great!" He growled turning to Venom. "Good bye"

At that Darkne reached into the air and posed his hand as though gripping a dial he then turned it like an invisible thermostat and Peterson started to go red, his skin bursting all over and boiling, flesh falling away from the bone leaving small sizzling scraps laying blackened and smouldering on his melting bones, steam poured from his eyeballs as a white liquid ran down from the sockets, Peterson had opened his mouth to scream but all this did was let loose even more steam, his teeth were no more, his hair was scorched off and half his skull was showing, even that was singed and turning to water.

Venom had withdrawn from his burning friend and was covering his eyes a wailing sound escaping from his lips. Peterson was reduced to a pile of smoking ash and raw red muscle sprinkled with broken half melted bones.

"So then Venom, would you like to have that kind of power? To be able to create human pâté?" Chuckled Darkne. Venom stood upright shaking with grief and anger.

"You EVIL bastard!" He roared

"Yes a lot of people call me that but I know they all secretly like it" Replied Darkne, Venom charged yelling a curse, Darkne grabbed his wrist and pulled him up over his shoulder then letting go, the Viper was sent flying across the classroom unable to stop until he came into contact with the wall. With a thud Venom landed on his arse, his back slamming against the wall.

Thomas started towards his defeated opponent laughing a malevolent cackle, stepping slowly past the desks which covered the cowering children. Darkne raised his hands by his sides and smiled showing his yellow, rotten teeth. A red smoke rose from the ground and tangled around the children

"NO! Leave the children alone! They haven't done anything wrong!" Venom pleaded, unable to move

"I know, isn't it heartbreaking? Poor innocent children" Darkne purred cocking his head to the side. The red smoke started to creep up the children's bodies wrapping its gas like tentacles around their arms, legs and necks, strangling them. The children didn't move; they just sat there under the tables staring emotionlessly at Venom with wide, dead eyes. The red visible gas covered them completely now in huge massing clouds. Darkne continued down the isle of tables drinking in Venoms defeated expression with great satisfaction. The children's flesh started to peel away as if the smoke was a swarm of man eating locusts nibbling away at the skin which was quickly turning to dust and falling to the floor. The skin was decaying; spreading like a plague through their bodies all that remained was the two dozen child skeletons still staring at Venom with white zombie eyes still bubbling away slowly. There was nothing Venom could do now except die and lose all his horrible thoughts and tortured emotions to the devil. But Venom was too stubborn to let death take him... so more hell was to come.

Chapter Thirteen: Miss Big guns

"NO!" Shouted the teacher from behind Darkne, he turned immediately.

"Yes sir?"

"Stop this madness!"

"Are you calling me mad? Well I am, I can't stop, it's an obsession, I love it" Darkne got out a steel, thin bar from his pocket and held it towards the teachers neck.

"Stop it!" Cried Venom getting up halfway onto his knee, groaning in pain. Darkne swapped the bar between hands and picked up a chair breaking off the leg, without looking back he threw the metal chair leg backwards like a dart at Venom, it sliced right through his knee and kept going, pinning into the wall behind him sticking him to the spot.

Darkne spoke to the teacher again holding the metal bar up to his face

"Did you ever teach the children about the Egyptians?" He asked

"Erm yes... last year" He whimpered in reply

"Aren't they great? How they mummify the dead? Did you know they got all the organs out of the body through one cut? And that they rammed a bar up the nostril and hooked the brain out with it just so they didn't break the skull?" He mused flipping the bar into the air

"Oh no! Please don't!" Begged the teacher stepping backing, eyes wide with terrified understanding. Thomas held him in place then prepared the bar, placing it gently in the entrance of the nostril

"Here we go!" Darkne said grinning. "This wont hurt too bad!" He lied. He added a huge amount of pressure to the end of the bar and jammed it further up the nostril; the teacher screamed manically, blood gushing out of his nose like a demonic waterfall.

"I unfortunately haven't been gifted with the skill of the Egyptians, I'm just a bit more messy" Apologised Darkne forcing it up further until the bones snapped, the teacher cried in agony as blood and death filled his head, Darkne continued to add pressure sliding the bar up the nose into the brain, the teacher fell silent, losing all feeling.

"How wonderful!" Cheered Darkne letting the body drop to the floor, he placed his foot next to the bar which was still lodged in the mans brain, he then kicked it up even further, the metal rod sticking out of the other side of the brain and through the skull

"I always wanted to do that" He clapped, then spun on his heels to face Venom

"Ok then friend, I have to go now. See you soon" He said rushing out the classroom door after unlocking it.

He left Venom behind racing down the corridor and heading towards the main entrance or exit in his case. The double doors swung open revealing Samantha and her group of body guards, more importantly, her gun! Darkne skidded to an unexpected stop, actually for once too shocked to react. Samantha saw him, her eyes narrowing then without hesitation ordered her men back, they dived for their lives as she pulled the trigger. Out of the end of the massive gun there was a burst of blinding light then the shape of a three headed dragon appeared flying at Darkne followed by a tidal wave of electrical yellow smoke, the dragon heads intertwined around Darkne, holding him in place, he really actually struggled! Unable to break free of the powerful hold. The wave hit him with the noise of a sonic boom, the force of a giant's fist. His eyes exploded, his teeth shattered, his finger nails crumbled, his hair flopped down into his face, his smug, evil smirk was wiped away as well as his famous eyeliner and lipstick. His head hung; the rest of his body frozen.

"Sorry honey, but you aren't getting out of this one" Said Sam wiping a forehead of sweat away. The ghostly words 'Good girl' set in Darkne's tone drifted through the air like his twisted, beaten spirit escaping to the wind. Sam dropped the now useless gun, her shoulders slumping forward.

"Right," Sam gasped "Darkne is no more" out of breath after handling the intense power and strength of the magically advanced weapon. She let out a shaky, weak breath, not able to believe what she was about to say

"He's dead"

☐

☐

☐

Chapter fourteen: Deep grave

"It is in the very heart of the base, underground. Even if he did escape we would be able to recapture him" Said one of the men leaning across the table at Sam.

"He won't be able to escape" Corrected the other man

"We need to be absolutely sure of that" Sighed Sam.

"Well... we are" Nodded the first man

"You don't sound it"

"That's because even we are overwhelmed with how inescapable the place is" Replied the second man.

"How are you sure?" Asked Sam unconvinced. "What's stopping him from breaking through the bars?"

"Well, there is a magical fluid that runs around the bars, the subject can use magic inside the cage but not to contact anything outside of it. It's like a force field, any magic that tries to pass the steel bars is halted. If the subject tries to attack the bars they will reflect his magic back at him, the more he fights the more he gets hurt" Explained the first men proudly

"Ok, that ...sounds good" Sam concluded, with much surprise. "Ok, looks like we shall be using your cage"

The two men cheered and they shook hands, before Sam walked out of the doors happy to be outside again in the sunlight.

"Any news on why and how he's still alive?" Asked Vein, back at the D.S base as Sam returned.

"Cant I get through the door first sir?" She grumbled slinging off her leather jacket

"This is important Samantha!" Shouted Vein, proceeding towards her

"NO!" She snapped stopping him in his tracks. "I don't see how any one else could know if we don't!"

"Yes, this is a big mystery ... could you go and check on him?"

"Why cant you?" Argued Sam

"Because, Samantha, I am more important than you, I am the leader. You are just my minion." Spat Venom

"Ok lovey. But if he gets out and eats me you'll have no more arse to look at" Sam said before disappearing through a sliding door.

She walked down the white corridors passing many doors on her way that said weird things on them like 'Door 2: Eaters' or 'Door 3: feeders' and 'Door 4: Spellers' these names all meant something to Sam, they were different categories of magical spells, some people only had certain types of spells made available to them, all this place was was a giant freak show. Sam continued towards the huge double doors at the opposite end which were sealed with a deadlock/airlock. She reached them then placed her hand over the centre, her palm started to glow red and the whole door turned an orangey, bright flame colour. There were six long beeps then the doors slowly opened letting loose a massive blast of vacuumed air from inside. Sam stepped through. Surrounded by tall, steel bars with one inch gaps in between, stood an almost lifeless Thomas Darkne swaying to and fro like a zombie, his eyes were still missing and his mouth still lacked teeth, gums and a tongue. His normally spiked up hair was flat against his forehead, the blood used to style it was now dripping from the tips of the long black strands. A dim blue vapour waved around the bars coiling around them like never-ending serpents

"Hello Samantha" Greeted a voice from nowhere

"I hate that" Muttered Sam in reply.

"How can I talk when I lack a tongue, my cold, chapped, white lips don't move, I do not breathe?" Questioned Darkne's voice which seemed to be coming straight from the very walls around Sam

"You have a very talented magical soul... how do you manage to move... to eat-"

"How do you know I eat it?" Darkne asked sharply

"Well... simply because you don't have any meat left when we see you next after giving it to you, I guess you don't just magic it to dust?" Replied Sam

"Ok, couldn't I be doing something else with it?" Darkne hissed the question. Sam merely raised an eyebrow at that

"You feed me meat on a giant fishing hook like an animal, why would I oblige you by eating it?"

Sam stepped forward until she was just a metre away from his cage

"Because you ARE an animal!" She spat in disgust

"Why" Said Darkne slowly... calmly, he leapt forward at the bars, moving as a blur "DO I LOOK LIKE AN ANIMAL TO YOU!?!" He showed his fangs. Sam fell backwards with a yelp of shock and terror, smacking down onto her backside. Darkne stepped back to the centre of the cage and stood still, collected against, head hung, facing the floor. Sam; not bothering to get back up, gasped "How did you do that?!"

"Sometimes I build up my energy by not moving or saying anything just so I can use that reserved energy in short bursts just to scare your panties off" He explained simply.

"Answer me" Started Sam getting up cautiously now. "How come you are not dead?" The big question, Darkne was getting very bored of this question as he had been asked it on many awkward occasions... but never before from Sam.

"Well Samantha, I thought you'd never ask" Darkne said

"Well... what is the answer? Surely you can tell me" Pressed Sam backing away slightly, preparing for another attack from the unpredictable maniac.

"Ah, so you have noticed I have a soft spot for you. Well Samantha dear, why don't you answer me this? What is your real surname?" Darkne said changing the subject quite dramatically.

"I don't see how this matters, you can read my thoughts." She answered shortly

"Yes... yes I can. And you are feeling so on top of things at the moment don't you? You feel that you are dominant over me. Believe me when I say, you are not... on top... of things..." He trailed off, then Sam could almost hear him smirk with joy "Ahhhh... good" He purred as he felt her heart rate speed up and become more frantic.

"Answer me!" Sam ordered, her voice now shaking uneasily.

"Only if you do something for me first" Darkne proposed.

"What would that be?" She asked eagerly

"Bring down the defences of this base, help me escape. If you do I will tell you the answer and leave you alive, never to see you or bother you again. You know deep down that you can trust me."

Sam's eyes narrowed...

☐

☐

☐

☐

Chapter Fifteen: Snake out the cage

"Vein! Vein! Vein!" Cried Sam rushing to the door reading 'Number 1: The big cheese' the door crashed open slamming against the wall behind it. Vein jumped to his feet from off his chair as Sam raced towards him

"The Devils spell!" She gasped collapsing over his desk

"What?! Impossible!" Shouted Vein in disbelief. "Not even he would be powerful enough to withstand that kind of energy, the spell would have ripped him to pieces and eaten him alive" Veins eyes widened. "Unless he-"

"You don't really think he could be?" Questioned Sam gulping down hard.

"There's no other way to explain it, how else could he still be alive?" Shrugged Vein, Sam sat down on the other side of the desk.

"So what exactly is this spell?" She asked

"Ok, well, it was in a book, the "Chicago Murderer" A huge, black book shaped like a melted spider"

"Why the 'Chicago Murderer'?"

"I have no clue, another mystery. But the book contained one huge, long spell. That was it. A spell that was kept in a massive book, crazy! It must have taken ages to perform. The spell is so powerful it's hard to record and know what it does. The legend is, if you can handle the power you become impervious to death, not invincible...it's always specifically said as 'impervious to death'." Vein explained

"I can't really see a difference"

"I know, but that's what it is" Sam thought for a moment, her face scrunching up as her brain churned through the information.

"So… perhaps that suggests there is a way of killing him? Or maybe defeating him at least, to render him powerless? To get the better of him? Maybe it's some kind of riddle… why else would it specify 'Impervious to death' and not just come straight out and say invincible?"

"There are many things we do not know and cannot hope to know about this spell and the power it grants but what is told is that the spell is supposed to kill anyone too weak to take the strength of the magic. The spell has the power of the devil, all Satan's power is poured into your brain after you cast the spell. Most people say it was all just a stupid trick, as you'd have to actually BE the devil to be strong enough to cope with it. So apparently if Darkne has survived it he is as strong as the devil" Finished Vein

"Bloody hell!"

"Exactly"

Darkne told Sam the story of how he cast the spell. He said he bought the book at the age of seven at a boot fair just because he liked the shape. His mother didn't like it, she hated it in-fact so he had to hide it in his room so she never found it. Young Thomas got out the book one day when he was bored and read out the words, doing all that the book told him to do. Little did he know that it could have killed him. After that he was living with the power of Satan himself flowing through his veins, un-killable for the rest of his life.

Darkne waited until he was alone in his room then unhooked his meat from the hook which was slid through the bars of his cage from the outside. He waited patiently as the camera turned to the side to scan the rest of the room leaving Darkne in its blind spot for a second or two, he darted across the cage to the back wall, there were no bars there just six metres of solid concrete. Darkne swiftly opened up a door in the wall which he himself had made with his nail and placed the meat amongst the other rotting, rancid smelling bundles. He then closed the wall back up and sealed the cracks with a magical paste just before the camera turned back of course seeing nothing suspicious at all...

In the watch room, amongst the TV's displaying the many different camera angles a D.S stood up staring closer at the one single camera screen displaying Darkne's room.
"Something's up" He grumbled to his colleague.
"What? I can't see anything"
"Look" Said the man pointing to the edges. "The camera is shaking slightly as it moves back and forth" All of a sudden the men fell silent as the screen cut off... a black, blank screen...
"VEIN!" They thundered in sync.

Vein burst through the doors of Darkne's room followed by ten armed guards with purple glowing machine guns and Sam who held a chainsaw.

"READY! AIM-" Shouted Vein cutting himself short as he saw no harm was done, there was no need to expect the worst... the camera was off the wall and smashed on the floor but Darkne was still in his cage, no one else was in the room

"Ah... well it must have... fallen off, he can't reach it using magic" He tried to reassure himself.

"Get another camera in here this second" Then he spotted Darkne's empty giant fishing hook and added.

"Oh and feed this thing some more" The armed guards left the room seeing no danger within, Sam and Vein remained watching the two men place a large steak on the hook and sliding it through the bars.

"Well looks like there's-" Vein was interrupted by the door of a locker swinging open from the corner of the room, the one that contained the electro stick. A black blur flashed across the room and tore into the back of one of the feeders. He fell, his backbone jutting out his skin, roaring in agony. The next feeder turned but was pounced on by the black haired figure; his throat was ripped out and thrown across the room in seconds. The first man scrambled across the floor with his bones cracking as he went, his hand went for the bars of Darkne's cage trying to get up. The wolf from behind him padded over his body sticking its paw through the hole in the man's back. It

256

bit down into the man's head and he stiffened. Darkne snatched the keys from the feeders wrist.

"Jesus Christ!" Cursed Vein who had been frozen to the spot in shock the entire time.

"Get the guards back in here now, how did that wolf get in here?!" He was shouting franticly with confusion and anger, Sam nodded and rushed out to get back up leaving Vein alone in the room of death. The cage door opened with a brain curdling screech and the wolf disappeared as Darkne clicked his fingers stepping out of the cage "You silly boy Vein" He said still missing his teeth and eyes. As Vein turned to flee out of the room; his only option possible, Darkne clapped his hands together and the double doors locked with a hiss trapping Vein in the room with him. Vein's hand began to glow but Darkne stopped him, lifting him up into the air. He slammed him back down against the floor crushing his legs, Vein wiped his hands across them trying to heal them quickly. Darkne pulled out his metal pole from his inside blazer pocket and produced a small tube of superglue. Opening his mouth wide; he would have been grinning, "Skinning time!" He said.

☐

☐

Chapter Sixteen: RIP Vein

A yellow and white light surrounded Darkne acting as a tornado around his body, circling his limbs. Thomas rose into the air, his bare feet flexing in the breeze created by the wind of the magic. When Darkne landed he had his teeth and eyes back in place.

"That's better" He sighed staring at Vein "Are you sitting comfortably?" Vein tried to get up from the floor but only froze half way, yowling in pain. His skin was still attached to the floor, Darkne had super glued him to it using magic

"Now, hold still" Said Darkne as he placed a blob of glue on the end of the steel bar moving it towards Vein's face

"How did this happen?!" Gasped Vein

"Well if you're sitting comfortably… I was stealing your steaks and sticking them in a secret compartment in the wall" He began, pointing to the wall in his cell, the rip fell open and the rotting meat rolled out like a giant rockslide.

The disgusting smell filled the air and forced Vein to gag sickeningly, Darkne however didn't seem to notice.

"I'll continue… My lovely pet Fang could smell the stinking stink from his domain and came to my aid like any loving animal would. Your pathetic excuse for a cage only blocked out magic, you were so obsessed with stopping that and other unnatural presences that you forgot all about the more natural and normal ways of escaping." Explained Darkne with dark pleasure, tossing the steel bar up like a

258

baton.

"I can hardly agree that your pet dog coming to save you because of a smell is totally normal." Vein argued

"Well of course when I first got Fang as a cub I altered his DNA and made him magically enhanced, bettering hearing, better smell, not that he smelt bad… better sight and better walking through wall abilities" Darkne finished, grinning.

"Wolves can't walk through walls normally" Noted Vein

"Well you can't expect me to do anything that doesn't include at least a little bit of magic" Quoted Darkne

"No, not if you're you, if you did anything without magic you'd drive yourself-" He obviously realised how stupid he would have sounded and stopped himself completing the line

"There, now you know my story I can kill you" He gurgled thrusting the metal bar at Veins arm, the glue end to his skin.

"NO!" Screamed Vein his eyes almost popping out of his head. Darkne pulled the bar down his arm and the flesh pulled away like a banana skin showing the red, pulsing muscle beneath. Vein went to roar out but Darkne kicked him down, the rest of his body gluing upon contact to the floor.

"Oh god no, leave me alone!" Squealed Vein trying to lift his head; his hair disconnecting from their roots. Darkne pulled the bar up breaking the rest of the skin off his arm, it dangled over Vein on the end of the steel pole. Darkne fed himself like a child with spaghetti then bit it from the end of the bar leaving it bare. He licked his lips.

"Just like Donna kebab!"

"For god sake stop this!!" Vein pleaded pathetically.

"You should know by now, the more you struggle the more I hurt you, and it doesn't seem likely that you'll stop struggling anytime soon." Darkne replaced the glue with another fresh glob and jammed it to Veins foot, his toes stiffened trying to brace themselves just as Darkne ripped the bar upwards tearing the sock of skin away showing the white bones of each of his toes. Vein let out another chorus of yells and went still. Darkne stepped over him as if going for the doors, leaving Vein alone for once… but that was only a dream and instead Darkne let go of the bar just as he stepped over Vein's head, the pole plummeted down and punctured Vein's eye, slicing through his skull then finally his brain. Now Darkne left, walking through the double doors.

Sam was rushing up the hall of white, yelling for help, D.S Soldiers filing out the doors around her, wielding huge machine guns and racing to Vein's aid, not yet aware that it was far too late. Sam must have known he was dead but she was just trying to slow down Darkne's progress towards her. The situation she was left in was, Thomas Darkne stuck in a base full of men who don't appeal to him and her, who is a perfectly good slab of meat in his eyes, she knew that she was his main target now. She reached Venom's ward, he had been regenerating himself on a magically advanced medical bed, recovering after the fight with Darkne and the knee/chair leg incident. He was also getting his fingers placed together again. Sam barged through the door and ran to Venom waking him up from a state of deep meditation ending the recovery leaving him with still his right middle finger missing; the one of the two fingers bitten off by Darkne.

"What?! What's happening?!" He mumbled sitting up suddenly staring around the room half blind and shivering, he had to shut down his body for the medical treatment so it would take a while for his natural senses to come back completely.

"Its Samantha, you've just woken up from a deep meditation. But we've got to move now!" Sam said worried, trying to push Venom over to the next door that led further away from the centre of the base and Darkne.

"OK! OK! Wait a minute." Venom was talking as though drunk as his mouth didn't work all that fast as if numb. He hopped off the bed and clumsily kicked his feet into the black boots he always wore.

"Darkne has escaped from his cell" Shouted Sam to Venom trying to hurry him

"What?! You didn't kill him?!" Roared Venom obviously something had sparked off in his brain

"NO, the gun didn't work as well as we thought it would. We only half killed him" Explained Sam pushing Venom towards the door

"But why did you lock him up? That was only going to make him angry with us, now you've given him a reason to kill us!"

"But Vein insisted we capture him, we were certain he wouldn't escape"

"Of course he was going to escape, he's an evil genius! Oh you idiots!" Cursed Venom stepping through the door

"I was only following orders! I didn't want him in this base either!" Sam said in defence sending Venom forward further. "Now GO!"

"Ok, it's not your fault but it doesn't matter, we're still going to die in this hell hole." Cried Venom

"We can fight, we're going to the best place for a fight to the death" Venom let Sam go off ahead following her now, he stared at her from behind.

"Ok Sam, you saved me before, my brain was about to turn to flamed jelly in that watery oven and you saved me just in time. The least I can do is blow Darkne's head off with you" He said sighing. "I've got nothing to lose now, the last time I faced Darkne in a real confrontation I had the lives of my whole base in my hands. Now I only have you to look after" He paused as they entered a smaller room with bright red lights dotted around the grey bricked walls. Sam pulled out a gun from a massive silver box and turned to face Venom

"You'll be looking after... *me?*" She questioned, smirking

"I'll take that back" Laughed Venom. "Ok, we'll fight Darkne to the bitter end and even if we do get killed terribly at least we're gonna make him very very sore!" Bellowed Venom, feeling like a twenty year old again.

Chapter seventeen: Darkne fodder

Darkne stepped down the narrow corridor of white, his strides high and majestic as he made steady, slow progress down towards Sam, his dinner. Eyeing the walls up ahead with caution he blinked then stopped, his hands swinging by his sides flinching.

"Come out from your hiding places boys" He called knowingly, his voice echoing down the hallway. The double doors on either side of the corridor ahead of him crashed open, thousands of armed guards filed out blocking the thin passageway. They were shouting orders and battle cries as they charged out. They dropped to one knee and rested their guns against their legs aiming at a delighted Darkne. One of the men called out a command to the rest, the helmets they were wearing all had glass visors, they flapped them down protecting their faces from whatever they thought was about to happen next.

"READY!" Roared a voice and all at once the guns started to glow, not all purple but different colours, some were mixture of many, red, blue, green, gold, orange, all depending on the strength of magical potential.

"Any last words Darkne? Before twenty five bullets pin through your body followed by another and another and another wave?" Called the voice.

"Me? Last words?! I'm not going to die silly" Answered Darkne licking his lips eyeing each one of the soldiers in turn making them shudder and shiver with fear.

"Ok men, kill him, OPEN FIRE!"

Now it was obvious why the men were wearing visors, the bullets were whizzing past the heads of their comrades like crazy, all darting towards Darkne. In a flash he was gone and when the firing stopped he reappeared before them.

"Do you want to try again?" He asked, mocking them

"FIRE!" The voice came again.

This time Darkne winked and as the bullets left the end of the nozzles of their guns they exploded, the blast ripping off the ends and making them useless. Some of the explosions knocked the men's helmets off and the bullets that weren't affected collided with the back of the heads of the people in front, blowing them to pieces. A grenade sailed above the heads of the men followed by another net of them soon after, it went quiet, silence ensued, all eyes pinned on the grenades in front of Darkne's feet. He waved a hand at them and they let loose an explosion, instead of a powerful blast of magical energy a glorious mass of blood was sent flying out in a display, much like fireworks.

The soldiers ahead of him were very worried now, but still they wouldn't, couldn't, give up. They readied another blasting session but stopped short, they had to reload! Darkne saw his chance; the army of losers saw the end. Darkne lifted himself into the air floating on a red cloud of destruction.

"Now boys, you will witness my wonderful finale, you are the main entertainment" He chuckled. A storm of white gas rushed through the men then was gone almost as quickly as it had appeared. Nothing seemed to have happened until the soldiers felt a black liquid running down their arms. Their guns had turned to acid which was now climbing up their shoulders and eating away at their skin, the blackish water froze, stopped moving and then turned solid again. The men's bodies stiffened, dead. Silence once again in the deathly hallway as Darkne strolled towards them knocking into them as he passed, snapping parts of the ice sculptures off.

"And now, a lovely orchestra to end it" Darkne purred to himself as he clicked his fingers adding life back to the statues followed by nothing but screams.

Sam and Venom stood in the centre of the room, Sam holding her own personal "Big gun" and Venom holding a thick, metal coated blade that ended as a sword but had a spear welded onto the end as well, a hybrid, created to do double the damage. Sam would have to put her magical energy into it for Venom to actually make it worth while but still it looked ugly enough to do the trick.

"He should be here soon" Said Venom.

"He's never been one to miss a date" Added Sam aiming her gun at the only way in. Her gun was all ready to go, glowing with a purple aura.

"Ok I'll do yours in a sec" She said looking over at Venom's dull spear/sword, her eyes increased by twice the size as she started to splutter and point franticly at the weapon hanging in Venom's grip.

"Venom!" She gasped jumping around on the spot like a freak.

"What? I heard you, you'll do me next"

"There's no need"

"Yes" He snapped impatiently. "To kill Darkne it needs to be magically-"

"NO! I don't have to do it!" Shouted Sam annoyed

"Ok, right so... how the hell do you expect-"

"NO! LOOK! Your weapon!" Sam said pointing at the spear headed sword, Venom looked down,

"OH JESUS!" He boomed, amazed, staring in disbelief at his sword spear which was already glowing a bright, ruby red.

"That's the highest mark of magical energy!" Yelped Sam.

"What's doing it?" His mouth hanging open dumbly.

"YOU!"

"But, I'm not doing anything!" Argued Venom.

"But... you must have had the magical potential within you all along and... the meditation! The meditation! You awoke your magical spirit with meditation!" Sam screeched

"So... I'm a magician!?" Venom asked, eyes widening with growing understanding, remembering when Darkne shared a message with him, Venom felt a surge of energy flow into him when Darkne stared into his eyes. He had somehow stolen magical powers off Darkne!

"I know how-" Venom started to say but was interrupted by a horrible hissing voice from outside the door.

"Little pigs, little pigs, let me come in"

Chapter eighteen: One down, one to go

The metal door fell apart around Darkne's feet as he stepped
through the empty doorway

"Hello piggy's"

"It's you" Venom said as calmly as he could. Sam shuffled forward a
few steps

"Yeah hi" She then lost it and sent an array of bullets at Darkne.
"NOW DIE!!!!" She bellowed desperately. The purple metal didn't
stop like expected; it instead actually pierced his flesh! Darkne
collapsed onto his knees, the bullets pounding into his body,
shattering his defences

"Now that's bloody painful" Shrieked Darkne, biting his teeth down so
hard the top set ground past the bottom and sliced through his lower
lip. Blood shot out like a fountain from his mouth all over the floor in
front of him. He dropped to his hands and knees then spat up blood,
staring at the mess before him. For some miracle of a reason he was
somehow caught off guard. He bled from many bullet holes in his
chest like a normal human being

"How does that feel?" Asked Sam standing above him, she kicked
him and he collapsed onto her boots

"How long ago did you actually feel pain?" She spat. "Hurts don't it?"
At that point Darkne stood up in a final burst of rage and
overwhelming power to kill her and Venom in a second. Venom leapt
in front of Sam slicing his sword/spear through Darkne's stomach. It
opened a huge gapping hole in his body, he dropped over

backwards with the weapon still lodged in his guts. Still he managed to talk.

"So you've finally found out how to use your magic?" He sounded slightly happy for a dying man.

"Yes, too bad for you" Replied Venom "This is where it ends!"

Darkne struggled out a weak gurgled laugh.

"What will we do with the body?" Asked Venom turning away from the bloodied death scene, when he got no answer he sighed before turning back to see a room tainted with tragedy.

"Leave us alone! Die properly like any other decent human being!" Thundered Venom seeing Darkne holding Sam by the throat. The sword spear was half way across the room and the massive hole in Darkne's body had already sealed up again

"It really doesn't take me long to regenerate, you know me" Growled Darkne, still dripping with blood but a lot better now then a few minutes ago.

"So, next victim and this one is a real prize... how should I kill this one Venom? Any ideas?" He questioned eyeing up Sam's bare neck, watching the blood pump through her big, juicy vein

"Just..." Venom tried to collect himself. "Put her down, leave us alone, why do you need to kill us?" Darkne's grip tightened around Sam's neck

"Why, I can give you a whole list" Began Darkne sniffing his victims hair.

"First of all… you hunted me down, you became interesting to me, you have survived for ages already, you betrayed me at the date we had, you killed my kiddie puppet, you're a Viper, you stabbed me, and when you thought I was dead you were going to throw my corpse away like a piece of rubbish. I want to kill Samantha because… she is very edible, she shot me with the mega whatever gun, she stuck me in a cage, she didn't talk to me like a nice woman, she called me an animal, she shot me just now, and most of all I just cant let her get away without bursting that lovely, appealing jugular in that neck of hers." Finished Darkne without a breath

"Oh…ok" Venom said, hopelessly.

Darkne moved like lightening towards Sam's neck slicing it open as easily as a piece of string. He clamped his lips around the wound and sucked down the blood like a thirsty leech. Venom knocked Darkne aside with a ball of magic which he couldn't understand and caught Sam in his arms. She was losing a lot of blood as it gushed out of her neck continuously, never stopping like a river of red gore. Venom placed his hands over her neck and prayed to god before pushing down, feeling a jolt of magic shoot through his fingertips. Sam grabbed a mouthful of air with her parched lungs and latched onto it like hell, her neck was sown back together within a second before too much damage was done. Venom then stood facing Darkne and sent twin balls of flame at each of his arms, Darkne simply snorted and waved them away, putting them out before they got anywhere near. Venom cursed as Thomas closed in then anxiously created two more flames from his palms before shooting them directly as his chest, they conjoined half way there and buried themselves into their target but nothing happened, Darkne just smiled, lunged forward, grasped his claws round Venom's throat then with the other hand punched his arm which disconnected at the elbow upon impact. Venom struggled pathetically, Darkne tutted in disappointment before snapping his second arm off then tossed him aside ready to claim his female prize. Venom went to intervene but all his strength had left him, all he could do was groan and watch sorrowfully.

Darkne was just above Sam when she made her move, she got to her feet in a split second and produced a giant bubble of magic that pulsed around her as a protective shell. Darkne sighed then let his body sag.
"It was nice playing with you Samantha, but now it seems it is the end"
She blinked back at him.
"What do you mean? Even you can't get through this as easily as you'd like" Her eyes flicked nervously side to side, not quite as confident as she'd like.
"I don't have to" He replied simply then directed his palm to her, face staring at the floor. The defensive bubble of magic surrounding Sam stopped pulsating and then nothing…. Seconds later it was closing in on her, her eyes widened
"What are you doing?!" She shrieked

A half smile appeared on Darkne's lips

"Why, killing you my dear" As the previously protective shield began to press tight against her skin all Sam could say was…

"Oh" Before her bones began to poke out of her skin.

Chapter nineteen: The missing Phone call

Venom dragged his body uselessly across the floor, no longer able to use his arms which hung off his elbows trailing blood in twin streams behind him. His eyes pale white, filled with anguish as he stared hopelessly at Samantha's body which was slowly imploding on itself. Darkne turned to the Viper on the floor still holding his hand out in the direction of Sam, the twin bones in her left arm shot out spurting blood in separate directions, she screamed in agony, "Please make it stop!" No one in the room was sure exactly who she was directing that at.

"Sorry about this Venom. Has to be done, the numbers 6 and 6 mean something to you?" Darkne inquired, Venom's eyes flew open in recognition despite the intense pain

"The number!"

"Numbers" Darkne quickly corrected.

"The number you made me call!" Venom continued, "What is that about?! You must tell me everything!"

Darkne pursed his lips together simply and twisted away from Venom to focus fully on Sam whose skin was now tightening so much that she looked like a living skeleton, both arms now covered in blood but still pumping out gallons more. Her skin was creaking now, suddenly her ankle bones exploded outwards like clay pigeons her blood turning the bottom half of the bubble of magic into a paddling pool, her screams echoed off the walls, rocking the room itself.

"Beautiful isn't it?" Darkne hummed to himself

"I'll kill you!" Venom snarled in reply, hatred fuelling his slow, pained approach; he was about a metre away from Darkne now. The dark magician spun round viscously without warning and laughed hysterically, his eyes alight with evil glee.

"YOU!? You really think you can kill me?! Your powers are nothing, I gave them to you, I could take them away!"

"No… I stole them from you!" Protested Venom, even as he said it he knew it was false

"Of course…" Darkne grinned menacingly. "Did you honestly ever believe you could have taken power from me without me knowing? ME?!" Venom made a bemused face that gave him the answer, not that he needed it.

"Oh you poor fool, I gave you my powers, but not as a gift, that part of the whole thing was more a… side affect. I was cursing you Sarge" His razor sharp teeth glinted as he pulled them together into a giant monstrous grin, at that Sam let out another chorus of screams as her shin bones snapped in half and jutted out of her flesh protruding awkwardly stretching the skin that had already began to tighten back around the loose shards of white.

"What? What does that mean?!" Venom snapped, blood still pouring from his half severed arms

"I'm sorry to say this my dear friend, but I kinda gave you an infection" His eyes shone a deep red. "I cursed you, so now for as

273

long as you live everyone you draw near have not even the slightest chance at living long, fulfilled, happy lives. Say good bye to your loved ones… forever!"

Something deep down inside Venom sparked off and he jumped to his feet in a flash, teeth bared launching himself at Darkne.

"You BASTARD!" He thundered, he crashed into Darkne to no affect and just slid to the floor, tears in his eyes.

"You can't do that… you can't do that…" He trailed off and stared at the floor.

"I can and I already have" Muttered Darkne in answer.

Sam's screams and howls of agony were now just a long never ending tune which changed dramatically in tone whenever another bone pierced through her body,

"PLEASE!!" She screeched as her ribs started to pop one at a time, cracking and crunching as her chest forced itself to meet her back bone.

"Please don't let this happen!" her teeth shattered, her collar bones separated and speared her shoulders, her skull hugged her brain and began to squeeze turning her screams to high pitched squeaking noises but still Darkne could not allow her to just die, not just yet.

"NO!! It's all your fault!!! Kill yourself now!!!!!!" Venom's heart stopped… Sam's brain collapsed in on itself as her last screams rung through the Vipers head   "IT'S ALL YOUR FAULT!!"

He couldn't move, he couldn't even attempt to stop the last

remaining blood drops draining out of his body, Sam was dead and he was next, Darkne had won, and Venom couldn't do anything about it.

Sam's body was now a mushed pile of shattered bones and scraps of skin, she was dead because of Venom and so would anyone else be who got close to him if he allowed himself to live on past that night, but he wouldn't have to worry about that, he could feel himself drifting away. His body was almost an empty shell, free from sadness, free from pain, free from guilt, free from everything. Death was approaching, reaching out its mangled claw, the nails on its fingers just inches away from his soul, and he welcomed it…
"No no no no no" Darkne purred, his finger tips brushing over Venom's dying heart, light came rushing back, blood pumped through his veins, emotions flooding into his rotten carcass, he could move again.
"NO!" Venom roared throwing himself at Darkne, he was tossed to the ground again. He brought his hands up to fire magical blasts but Darkne snorted and the glow died almost instantly. Venom then gave up, his entire body sagging, he slumped to his knees.

"Why?" He cried bitterly "Why can't you just kill me?"
Darkne crossed the room and placed a hand on Venom's shoulder then sighed.
"You are not supposed to die just yet, I haven't done with you, but

don't worry" He winked. "I will kill you some day".

"I could just kill myself" Venom mumbled without much conviction.

"Yes… yes you could" With that Thomas Darkne gave a short laugh and stepped over the demolished pile that used to be Samantha, he gave a swift glance back, a smile then added

"I have a feeling we'll meet again"

The end…

That is all from the Vipers but next up

"I'm the good guy"

… … …

Finally I would like to thank Vic! For all the brilliant holidays he took me on where I wrote the majority of these stories! Yeah…holidays so brilliant I spent most of my time writing! Just kidding, they were honestly great! I'm just a bit weird, thanx xxx

Bonus Features Three:

Wow, glad that's all over? Well it's not! My next book will be out some time soon because OF COURSE I've already written it! The next book will be moving on with something completely different but don't worry, I promise you Venom will be back… at some point, thank you all so much with sticking through with it until the end, it's been a pleasure writing for you, no… YOU specifically.

Fun Facts

- *D.S stands for demon slayer, they weren't all just detective sergeant's! You'll be hearing more about those later on…*

- *Vein was named after one of my favourite characters from 'Lord Loss' Look it up!*

- *I actually had the ending of this book planned from the end of 'Trails of death'*

- *You will also be hearing more about the 'Chicago murderer' later on so don't worry if you didn't quite get that bit…*

Now here's a bit of homework I did for college once, it's 'Love hurts' In the style of a Grimm's brothers tale. Just thought it would be fun to put it in…

Red for Redemption

One day a dark and sinister witch cursed a new born baby with a terrible disease. This child grew up to become a very troubled teenager, the school bullies picked on him a lot and one day it got so bad that he came all the way home from school crying to his mum.

His mother however was not too comforting, she was angry that he had come home so late at night, she was worried sick but all she could do when he came in was shout and scream and screech at him. The small boy was so distraught he could not take one more minute of people shouting at him, something inside him snapped and he reached for a knife from a nearby knife block. He turned to his mother and shrieked manically as he drove his blade through her,

> Slice, slice, slice
> Slash, slash, slash
> Swipe, swipe, swipe
> And she was no more then chunks on the floor!

The poor boy ran away, from that house, has never come back, till this day.
He hid underground, and when the police came around, he was nowhere to be found.

What the witch had done when the boy was born, was cast a spell of which is worn on the boy forever more, a spell that allows him to raise hell to every human being, boy or girl.

One day it happened that he came back to the surface and set out to find the troublesome bullies. No one around would know who he was, so no one around would be found.

He arrived at the bullies house and using his magical potential he attacked them manically, with long held rage, and strength that had been granted throughout his age.

> Slice, slice, slice
> Slash, slash, slash
> Swipe, swipe, swipe
> And they were nothing more then chunks on the floor!

After this he said who's next? He had killed who he said, but still was vexed.
He killed and killed and drank the blood that spilled
The death count filled and filled but that was no more the better, he was still not thrilled.

He had a scar on his face, tall, black, spiky hair, yellow teeth, pale white skin, thick black paint round his eyes and nails and lips and heart, a gruesome, ugly character but he killed on and on carrying the name Thomas Darkne, life long tormenter!

But this was not how the story ends, for a helping hand the witch, she lends.
Along his way came Valerie who made him happy and gay,
She led him around with much dismay… let us see how the scene does play.

"Hello Valerie" Darkne said.

"I thought you would have forgotten my name by now"

But because of Darkne's magical gift he hadn't, the witch was already feeling cheated, her curse to him was more of a present. He said:

"No, how could I forget a name as lovely as that?" He warms his hands up magically and they walk together towards a limo which seems to appear as if by …..magic!!

Darkne opens the doors automatically, Valerie says.

"Clever doors!"

Darkne fills the car with red and pink lights, Valerie says.

"Clever lights!!"

Darkne made the car fly up into the sky, Valerie says.

"Oh my!!!"

Darkne glides a chocolate piece from a box into her mouth, Valerie says.

"You're a special guy!!!!"

Their lips touch and they embrace, nothing can compare... it says on Darkne's face.

"Who are you?" Valerie asks

"Your life long lover"

"Oh, at last!"

Everything is grand, what could make it bland?
Maybe just... what the witch has planned!

The limo lands, the doors open by hand.
Green and black takes over the room, sets it in darkness and in gloom.

Everything is confusion, then it's solved,
As soon is obvious, the witch is involved.

"You think he's perfect, but he's not,
He's killed people, and a lot!"

As the witch reveals Darkne's horrid, terrifying past, Valerie weeps

"This cannot last! If this is true.... I thought I loved you!!"

Darkne breaks down.

"But you do, and I love you too,
I've stopped the killing for the love that is due!"

Valerie stares hard and with thought.

"If that is right, there's no need to fight
I loved you once, and I just still might!"

The witch cackles with outrageous disbelief.

"But he's killed!! And that's not bright!!"

With these words she takes flight, the limo sets aflame, gives them a
fright.

The fire crackles madly with much bite. The lovely couple look, nod, and say
"Alright!"
Darkne and Valerie join together, and blast her and her flames away with a love that will last forever.

So that is the rule to this story, yes it does have a moral, even if gory.
If someone has done wrong but they mean to right,
then give them another chance, and they just might
Ignore the lesson or reject this story and I'll have to...

> Slice, slice, slice
> Slash, slash, slash
> Swipe, swipe, swipe
> And I'll make you nothing more then bloody,
> gory, chunks on the floor.

Thomas Darkne and Valerie Darkne lived happily ever after and Thomas vowed on their wedding day to never kill ever ever again... and he still hasn't... but it's just a matter of when!!

The End!!!

Now with nothing else to say I leave you with a preview for the next book and say good bye! See you   soon!...

I'm the Good Guy!

"A red spark of evil glinted in his eye as he outstretched his hand, a purple glowing light massing in his sweaty palm. He waved his other hand over the cowering group of civilians, a bunch of ravenous tiny snakes breaking out of his flesh. All his victims to him were merely prey. He stepped forward about to unleash his power on the humans, laughing manically then suddenly he froze, blood gushing out of his mouth like a waterfall. He looked down, eyes bulging. A set of long black nails clawed their way out of his stomach shining gloriously in the blood. The claws shot back out of his back and he slumped to the floor. The magician's captives stood, sighing in relief. Their savior, with black painted eyes and long, black, blood riddled hair … Thomas Darkne!!"

Printed in Great Britain
by Amazon

15734516R00163